Until Irene

A Novel By

A'taris Anthony

𝒟edication

This book is dedicated to all those who have been victims to natural disasters, and to my beautiful children Melanie, Aiden, Anquarius, and Anthony

Author Bio

Ataris Anthony was born July 17th, 1992. She is a former correctional officer who has observed and studied offender behavior. She began taking an interest in writing after serving 10yrs in the United States Army, and since has become a way of life. Until Irene is her first novel. This book was inspired by a tragic natural disaster that took away her home and gave her a new beginning.

A story based on true events.

Synopsis

When the storm of the century arrives in Paterson, New Jersey there are two young drug lords at war with one another and in an attempt to lay claim to every circulating dollar throughout the city's heroin distribution they will stop at nothing to eliminate the opposing competition.

Tommy Valentino and Curtis Crowder appear to be on a one-way trip to the city morgue, especially after a tragic accident takes the life of one of their most beloved. Tommy not only wants to murder his foes in as viciously of a manner as possible but is willing to take the life of all who stand in his way of avenging his sister.

With every intention of protecting his little brother, Curtis becomes the man that many fears he could in fact be and is on the verge of losing everything that he has worked hard to establish. Tired of playing the nice guy, he comes to the decision that everyone is game when it comes to war. He is ready to demolish any and every one that dares to contest him…even dirty cops.

While both the storm and the domestic battle progresses, the level of hostility rises to a feverish pitch that will cause some to plead for divine intervention.

In the end, the battle of a lifetime will become the largest victory for a city that never knew forgiveness... Until Irene.

Introduction

In the year 2011 one of America's most vicious natural disasters took the entire east coast by utter storm. Tearing its way through both large and minute cities like an enraged silverback gorilla with an insatiable lust for destruction.

Like never before, Hurricane season left an unforgettable amount of pain and anguish in the homes of many of our country's families, without any regards as to what race, creed, or financial classification its victims were in.

Indiscriminate winds and water claimed the precious lives of both old and young-strong and feeble. In just a matter of seconds, minutes, hours, and days billions of dollars were lost, as well as the hope, faith, and dreams of those who were already on the brink of accepting defeat at the game of life.

Time seemed to age a thousand years for some, leaving those who were determined enough to survive feeling old and withered, while for others it stood still, rendering them emotionally spent, lost, and in disbelief. Thousands did not care to live past the moment, unless they be forced to deal with the reality that they would have to rebuild what they had worked their whole lives establishing. Millions cried out for God's mercy, praying that chance bestow its blessing upon them.

When the sun hid itself behind the skies, and the winds screamed through the air like howling wolves, the rain gathered itself in puddles on the earth's surface and before long, turned the abandoned streets and freeways into rivers and eroded gullies.

Just twenty minutes from the great city that the world knew as the Big Apple; there was a war going on in a small town located in the North Eastern part of the state of New Jersey. No one but those that were involved knew the actual severity of it all. Like any other quarrel over local dominion the soldiers, warriors, and survivors of Paterson kept their beef with one another as discreet and restrained as possible, never allowing the authorities to catch wind. For some time, all had been kept under wraps; a scuffle here- a scuffle there. Maybe even the occasional stabbing, "occasionally". Then, just as the hurricane that would change the lives of many-even bring President Barack Obama out of the White House to comfort those in suffering- began to rear it ferocious head, the battered streets of an unprepared town were painted with the innocent blood of a young female child, causing the term hatred to take on an entirely new meaning.

No one in the city of Paterson, nor its surrounding areas knew what the gift of forgiveness actually meant, Until Irene. I present to you the story of how a natural disaster's destruction created peace in a domestic war.

Prologue

The streets of downtown Paterson were desolate. Unlike any other Friday afternoon, there were not many pedestrians moving about. No shoppers were roaming the area as would have been the usual on any other day. There were not any peddlers, there weren't any thieves, there were no window-admirers, nor were there any of the local beggars loitering at their usual posts. It all seemed so alien to the few business owners that refused to shut down their stores for the day, despite the weather forecaster's warnings that a horrific storm was on its way. Some believed that it just was not possible for a town such as their own to suffer a natural disaster; a storm that had never made its way into the city before. This was not the coast, so who could blame them. This was the ghetto. This was what some considered the slums. This was the home of Hurricane Carter, and Lou Coustello. Average people survived some of the toughest of times in this city. There was no way that some storm was going to come and steal that strength, pride, and self-assurance away from them. The people of Paterson were built like iron-they could survive anything. Resilience best described them as a whole.

Though, they were stubborn to the core, not many disregarded the angry-looking clouds that drifted hastily overhead, or the winds that whipped about like confused tornadoes. Nor did they ignore the vastly increasing raindrops that were beginning to pelt the Earth's surface like tiny pebbles of stone.

In just a matter of minutes, the amount of rainfall had increased rapidly, and the few that dared to contest the storm quickened their steps in search of shelter. Glancing around, you would have thought that you were in some sort of judgment day movie. The way that the sun seemed to cower behind the dark, distended clouds was somewhat mesmerizing. To the little twelve-year-old Caucasian girl who trudged her way down the abandoned sidewalk of downtown Main Street through the indiscriminately battering winds, it did seem like the world was indeed coming to an end. As a child, her mother had read to her countless stories from the bible and for some odd reason, the book of Genesis was a chapter that she'd never forgotten. The story about Noah and the Ark that he'd built at God's instruction appeared just as vividly in her mind now, as it had the very first time that her mother had read it to her. She could still see the deadly waters of the earlier times, as they flooded earth and did away with all that had defied God's commands. As she fought to contain her damaged umbrella, she tried to remember exactly what God had said to Noah after the flood had ended.

Had not he promised that he would never destroy the earth by water ever again, Alaena wondered, as she brushed her flailing hair from her face with the back of her free hand. Something about a covenant, she recalled.

To her left, she noticed an Asian man standing on the inside of his beauty supply store, staring through its large glass windows at her. She wondered why he was glaring so intently, but then she looked around and immediately understood... she was the only person on the entire strip unsheltered from the storm. Did not matter much to her, though, because she'd be home soon. She had only just eight more blocks to go and then she would be inside of the cozy confinements of the two-bedroom apartment that she shared with her older brother, Tommy. Alaena knew that once there, all of her crazy notions about God breaking his promise and putting an end to mankind once again would go away as quickly as they'd appeared, and tomorrow everything would be right back to normal.

Yes, Tommy will see to that, Alaena thought highly of her brother, who was her caretaker and the only male figure that she had in her life.

Reaching the corner's edge, she made a right turn and fought with her umbrella some more, just as the winds began to pick up. The rain stung more severely than before, and that's when Alaena noticed that it had begun to hail.

There was a crack in the pavement and misjudging her step, she stumbled and lost control of her umbrella. That is when she heard it… the sound… the strange screaming of a luxury vehicle's tires as they burned rubber and screeched harshly across the road's wet asphalt. Following that was something like the sound of a floor model television being bounced off a trampoline and crashing against the ground. Then came the loud balloon pops.

Regaining her balance, Alaena quickly glanced up. Her eyes held wide, she shot out a stiff hand to shield herself. The last thing that she saw was the cracked headlights of a black Mercedes Benz…then came the eternal darkness.

The music inside of Curtis' vehicle blared through the twelve-inch subwoofers, and six by nine speakers that sat in the door's paneling and rear window. The distinct vocals of a classic track by rapper Nas featuring Scarface flooded Curtis little brother, Lamont's ears as he nodded to the thudding base and tapped his fingers against the leather-covered steering wheel. A blunt sat perched between his pursed lips, as he contemplated the steps that he would need to take to reach the status of his older sibling. At the age of twenty-eight, Curtis ran the entire Westside of Paterson. He had the dope game on lock. Having been in the game for quite some time already, he'd managed to take the distribution of heroin to   another level. Raised by his foster mother in Queens, New York he'd grown up a poor black, snotty-nosed kid, and moving to the Christopher Columbus housing Projects in Paterson hadn't made it any easier for him. Yet now he was well on his way to becoming the first young black hustler from his click 'One-Two-Live' to actually make it up out of the ghetto wealthy, and unscathed. Problem was, now that he'd managed to stack up paper like those bodega coke dealing papis over in the city without catching any heat from the downtown crumb-snatchers called the cops, his younger brother 'L' began to want to follow in his footsteps in hopes of becoming the new Westside Neeno Brown. Lamont was always talking about running his own operation and being the general of his own click, but it was clearly all for naught, because he didn't have to. Curtis had already established all of that shit for them. Both his failures and successes in the game had made it to where, once their operation was shut down for good, no one left in the Crowder family would ever have to sell drugs again. They could go on and make something of themselves; maybe even go off to college. He'd love more than anything to be able to send Lamont off to school, somewhere in upstate New York. The young brother was only seventeen, anyhow. He had a long life ahead of him, just as long as he didn't do anything stupid.

Curtis on the other hand, had a little girl to look after. Besides his brother, his daughter was his main concern. She was his everything and the exact reason why in six more months he was kissing the business of heroin dealing goodbye. He was not about to let anything keep him from watching Shakira grow into the beautiful, young woman that he knew she'd become. Not even Lamont's overzealous ambitions to become some infamous hood-king. And his younger brother knew it. That's why he was currently driving through the afternoon storm with a furrowed brow, clearly upset.

Lamont was trying to block out the last discussion that he'd had just hours before with Curtis. His brother had been adamant in telling him that, no matter how much he felt offended, he would not support Lamont's efforts if he so chose to pick up his own bricks and pitch bundles, after all that he'd done to secure their future.

Out of anger, he'd snatched up the keys to one of Curtis' four vehicles and peeled out. Hadn't mattered much to Curt, though, because he'd made sure that 'L' had gotten his license just as soon as he'd come of age.

As Lamont sped down Broadway Avenue, the black 350 slicing through the winds like a hawk on its feverish hunt, he wondered how he'd be able to do this on his own, without involving his brother. Obviously, Curtis who was better known as Klick Klak, didn't think that he had what it took to be a king, so he was going to have to show him.

"Yeah, that's what I'll do. I'm gonna show him," Lamont declared through the loud music, after removing the blunt from his mouth to savor the smoke inside his lungs.

His cell phone began to vibrate on his hip, so he reached for it. "Shit!" he exclaimed at the sight of a kernel-size cherry jumping out of the tightly rolled cigar's enflamed tip. It fell onto his yellow and blue polyester Marquette basketball gym shorts, and instantly began to burn a tiny hole in the material. Frantically, he begun to brush at the burning fabric, and dropped his phone in the process.

"Damn it!" he said, and absentmindedly taking his eyes off the road, he bent to retrieve it. In that split second, the car jerked to the left. The tires screeched like they were in a world of pain, and hitting something that felt damagingly hard, the front two wheels exploded beneath him. Lamont never even got the chance to look back up, as he crashed into something unyielding and his entire world faded into a sickening blur.

1

At an arm's length, it was hard for someone to discern the actual reason for the obvious strain behind Tommy Valentino's eyes, but for his lady who was a continuous up-close and in-person, it was easy to see that the fatigue he felt was caused by the constant "beef" that he was undergoing with the black guy that ran the Westside of Paterson.

He'd complained to her time and time again about the decrease in his weekly product sales. Ever since the guy, Curtis, had dropped the cost of his bags of heroin from nine dollars to seven, it had become tremendously hard for him and his crew to compete with those prices. On a good day he was still pained to have to sell his bags for nine a pop. The way that his customer count had begun falling, you would have thought that he'd begun selling anthrax. The fact that his shit lacked a cleaner cut than that of his rival's didn't help matters much, either. It was like the motherfucker, Klick Klack was having his dope specially imported, or something. The competition between the two had become something of an unspoken declaration of war. No one cared to hear what the other had to say. Once that it had become apparent that the two and three dollar differences in the cost of product had begun to hurt the pockets of every Eastside hustler getting down with the 'D-Pound Crew', things had turned barbaric in a very unremorseful way. Guys from both money scheming teams were turning up at the emergency rooms with more stab wounds and head contusions than a New York City gang member from the 1800's.

Things were beginning to get out of hand, and Tommy knew that if Klick Klak didn't come to terms with him before long, and agree to distribute his heroin at a reasonable price, then someone was going to die before it was all over with. And in Tommy eyes, losing one or any amount of his soldiers was not an option.

Having been confided in more frequently as of late, Stephanie knew every detail of her man's troubles, and as she kissed him gently and looked into his eyes, she said a Hail Mary for him , before he exited their vehicle.

A Sicilian through and through, Stephanie had been raised as a Catholic and knew that adamant prayer could change anything. She loved her man very much and wished deeply that he'd change his lifestyle, because she didn't want to lose him to the streets, or the system. She wanted more than anything to marry Tommy, someday, because he was a good man, a family's man. The way that he was with his little sister was even more assurance that he'd be a great father whenever she bore him their first child. It was just getting him to see things her way that was the problem.

He'd talk, but he wouldn't listen. That was the one and only thing that she hated about him.

As Tommy turned and gave her one last glance over his shoulder, she wondered how soon or later this storm would be over. Both of the seen and the unseen. With his head hung low, and his navy blue New York Yankee baseball cap shielding his eyes from the few people occupying the neighborhood barbershop located on the corner of 17th and Park Avenue, Tommy checked both his pants and jacket pockets to make certain that he had on his personal all that he'd need for the next six hours. It was going to be a rough evening, with the rain not seemingly going to let up any, and with disgruntle demeanor he hoped to be able to get rid of several bundles before nightfall. It all depended on whether or not if those dudes on the Westside were as hungry and eager to make the extra pesos as he and his crew was. The weather was really beginning to be a bitch, and he hoped that most of the avid corner hustlers would choose to stay inside their cubbyholes and cuddle up with their female companions. That'd be more than enough to give him something to feel blessed about for the day.

Over the past month, things had gotten serious. Because of Klick Klak, his pockets were hurting and if things didn't change in Tommy's favor soon, then before long he'd be turning them out like rabbit ears.

Man, forget that, he thought, while standing on the inside of his man's shop, and watching intently as a few of his hustlers moved about in the rain-soaked streets. Shielded from the downpour by heavy black raincoats, they served several fiends who were in a desperate need of a fix.

Being one of the only white men that could actually say that they were born and raised on the rugged streets of Paterson, it wasn't odd to see the one that he had. He had grown up a natural born athlete, accelerating in both football and soccer like he'd been sired just for those purposes. That was until he'd discovered boxing. Deftly punching out someone else's lights had become his niche, and overall had gained him an irrefutable level of respect. After having been challenged by some of the most brawny and brazen brothers on his side of town and coming out victorious in nearly ninety-five percent of his fights, he'd acquired a rare status for Caucasian man raised in a predominantly Hispanic and black neighborhood. At the age twenty-five he had put together a solid entourage of gorillas that were thoroughly bred 'go-getters', as well. And thus far, every last one of them had proved to be loyal to him.

He had just been trying to remember the point in his life where his dreams and ambitions had been altered, and his promising career had been deferred, when Tony walked up behind him and placed a firm hand on his shoulder.

"Yo…you aiight, kid?" his friend for the past fifteen years asked. He could see the troubled expression on Tommy's face. Glancing at his middle-age protégé, tommy assured, "Yeah, Tone, I'm good. You know me… just contemplating on a million and one ways to rich."

"Yeah, I can dig that. Ain't we all…" the well-groomed black entrepreneur agreed. He dropped his hand and dug into his pocket. "You see this?" he asked withdrawing what appeared to be a buying this entire street out, and reconstructing the property for some fairgrounds bullshit," he said, discontent evident throughout his speech. He continued, as Tommy read silently. "Sonofabitches gone offer me that piece of chump change, and when I refused, they sent me that shit… talking about I don't have any choice but to accept their offer. Man, what the fuck's wrong with them?" he griped, his fists absentminded balling at his sides.

"This is my motherfucking neighborhood. I ain't going nowhere, my dude. Been here my whole fucking life…was raised on this street. They can suck my dick and the barrel of my steel if they think I'm budging," he declared.

Sighing, Tommy handed the letter back to Tony. "Damn, man, it's always something," he said shaking his head, and returning his sights back to the streets before them.

"Yeah, but it ain't shit I can't handle."

"What you mean? What you got planned?" Tommy asked.

"Man look..." Tony told him, "I know that it ain't nobody's doings but those motherfucking Italians. They been coming down here for the past two years talking about Al Chino wants everybody who owns a business in his neighborhood to start paying street taxes-ten percent of everything that we make. Every time they come around here talking extortion shit, I been puling that biscuits on they ass and running them the fuck off. Now Al Chino's uncle is the fucking mayor."

"You sure it ain't coincidental, Tone?"

Tony gave him a look that said 'man, please'.

"Aiight, so what you gone do?" Tommy asked, watching as another one of his pushers served customers who'd driven up in car. Amazingly, the rain had momentarily subsided. "I was hoping that you'd ask that, because there's something that I've been wanting to show you," he told Tommy, and they headed into the direction of Tony's rear office.

2

The darkness felt heavy, and all of the noises surrounding him were nothing less of a chaotic jumble of nuisances. Tiny green and yellow dots danced behind his eyelids, while biting winds and something else that he was currently unable to identify tore at his face, chafing his skin and causing a tremendously uncomfortable stinging sensation.

Nothing seemed to come to mind just yet, as Lamont tried figuring out exactly what was going on, and where he was. He wondered if this was some sort of bad dream, or just a badass reaction to some of the pills that he'd taken earlier that day. The thought that de could possibly be experiencing some deadly form of a bad trip disturbed him terribly.

Is this what a slow death feels like? He wondered.

Lamont began to cough and without warning, the slight expelling of the lungs turned into a jarring hack. When the heaving finally subsided, he could feel something wet dribbling from his mouth, and using the back of his hand, he wiped at whatever it was.

Willing himself to focus, he looked down and strained his eyes. Slowly, his vision began to reconstruct itself, and in a matter of seconds he could see the dark red blood on his arm.

Unconsciously, he began to breathe a little heavier than when he'd first awakened and in doing so a horrible jolt of pain travelled throughout his entire chest cavity.

"Agghh," he groaned, clutching a forearm to his badly bruised sternum. "What the fuck happened?" Lamont questioned when he noticed the broken gearshift. Those sharp pelts that he was continuing to suffer to his face brought his gaze back to the foreground, and the source of once of his many discomforts became apparent when he noticed that his windshield was shattered, and the large balls of hail that were raining down on him.

Immediately, reality struck him, and he remembered what had gotten him into this position. He'd been reaching for his cell phone that had fallen into the floorboard, when without warning the car had somehow been violently jerked to the left. The last thing he remembered before the utter darkness and the awakening pains was the loud screeching of his tires, followed by the teeth chattering clash of aluminum against stone.

Trying his door handle, Lamont was relieved when he found that he could easily climb out. He staggered out into the rain, before gaining his balance.

Taking a quick survey of his surroundings, he noticed that there were several store owners glaring out of their windows at him, yet none of them came to his aid.

Bewildered, he turned and began to scrutinize the damage that he'd caused to his brother's car. Taking several steps forward, his feet sloshed about in the large puddles of rain that were vastly becoming blackened by the oil leakage from the Mercedes' engine.

His breath caught and his eyes grew wide. Holding a shaky hand up to his chest, Lamont eased forward a bit more and stopped.

"Awe, nah, yo...come on!" he cried. "No. No. No... this can't be happening!"

He dropped to his knees, never minding his bare flesh against the wet pavement, so that he could get a better look. Reaching out, he touched the torn shoes of the female adolescent that lay lifelessly beneath the Benz. It was quite apparent to him that she was beyond saving.

Raising both of his hands, Lamont clutched his face and began to sob. He was scared beyond measure.

What in the fuck have I done? Curtis is going to kill me... he thought mournfully. Sirens could be heard approaching from somewhere in the distance.

Lamont wanted to stand...run...find somewhere to hide where no one would ever find him. He wanted to vanish... get missing and continue on living like this incident had never happened. At that moment, he wished that he could climb back into his mother's womb-never to be born… just stay there until life itself had no more existence. But as his body wracked in anguish, he knew that none of those options were possible.

Instead, he just stayed there crouched in that position, and pleading with God to return this little girl's life back to her. He was so traumatized by the accident that when the paramedics and the local police arrived. They had to literally pry him from the ground, before they were able to treat him for his injuries and begin their investigation.

Stepping inside of Tony's office, as usual, Tommy wondered how it was that such gigantic space could even be structured at the back of this establishment. It had to have been added on, or something. The room was unbelievable… designed to the tee. Its fit Tony's demeanor all too well.

The walls were painted a vibrant off-white. There weren't any windows, but the eloquent, artsy-craftsy décor that he had going on more than made up for the lack of outdoor visual.

At the far end of the room two separate furnishings for seating were stationed in opposite corners; a Vladmir Kagan Sofa, and a 'Big Easy' chair that Tony insisted was designed by someone of importance by the name of Ron Arad. There was a 1990 polished steel table designed by that exact same individual sitting oddly at room's center. Atop of it sat a Bronze Cubist Falcon by a Russian artist name Czaki. Hanging beautifully from the walls were two very large and expensive paintings, which were 'The Queen' by Tobias Keene, and another by Emmanuel Gondouin from the 1930's. The floor, though a well-kempt Timber, wasn't much, just your typical slats of glossed boards lain symmetrically beneath their feet. There were several throw rugs strewn about, and again Tommy wondered the reason behind the odd placements.

Despite the high outdoor humidity levels, back here it was as cool as an ice museum. As they made their way across the room Tony stopped abruptly at the steel table and laid a hand on the Falcon's head. Gripping it firmly, he gave it a slight twist and a faint clicking sound could be heard. Then, as if a hidden bank vault had been unveiled, a noise like that decompression invaded the humble silence, and a large section of the wall directly ahead of them gave away.

"Yo, what the fuck is that?" Tommy asked a bit bewildered, yet amazed. Tony said nothing at first, he just continued forward. Reaching the concealed barrier that was now held ajar, he glanced back over his shoulder. "Tommy, you know that I trust you, right?"

He asked, "Man, Tone, you know I'm." Tommy began saying, but never got to finish, because Tony turned back toward the large piece of wall that was actually a hidden door and pulled it wide.

It squeaked slightly on its hinges, then gave a faint thud when it smacked against the wall behind it. Tony stepped inside the dark space and flicked on a switch, illuminating the eight by fifteen size room.

"Oh, shit!" Tommy gasped at the sight of all of the shelved artillery. "Yo, what in the heck are you doing with all of this?" he asked in shock. There were guns galore inside of there. Never before had Tommy seen so many firearms at one time; all in the same place; all so close that he could just reach out and caress the cold steel of each and every last one of them.

Having rushed inside of the room, his senses picked up on the strong scent of gun powder and a faint smell of rusted metal.

There were several large chests lying at their feet and Tommy looked at Tony with a questioningly glare.

"Go ahead," he told him with a wave of his hand. Squatting, Tommy pulled the lid back on the one nearest to him. "Man, Tone, what in the world."

Inside there were neatly stacked fully loaded magazines, as well as boxes of ammo. He was amazed at how much weaponry Tony had stashed away inside of this secret room of his, and that he never even knew it existed. This was truly unbelievable to him. Here in front of them, was enough weaponry to start a motherfucking militia. Immediately, Tommy wondered what might happen if the wrong people ever found out about this room, specifically the local authorities. Surely Tony would be locked away inside of some federal facility for the rest of his life.

Finally, Tony spoke.

"This is what I've been doing with all of my money from the shop, and the extra cake that you hit me off with from time to time."

Tommy stood, still staring at his older friend in amazement. If he was honest with himself, he was actually in awe.

"At first..." Tony continued, "it started off as me just wanting to stack up some extra hammers to get off on... you know, maybe double-triple my money. But then those motherfucking fake ass politicians started bringing their asses around here with that bullshit. Tommy, I know they're deep. They're the mafia-they've got their own army, all away from the United States to Sicily. So, I've been equipping myself to start myself to start my own army, 'cause that shit ain't going down like that. Like I said, I've been here my whole life... I ain't goin' nowhere."

For a split second, Tommy was speechless. His level of respect for the old man skyrocketed. Had he known that this dude was as official as he was coming to learn, he would have been formed a team with him that would more than likely have prevented his current problems with Klick Klak and his crew.

A bubble of laughter escaped Tommy's lips. "Yo, what's up? What's so funny?" Tony asked, and a grin forming on his face. "I'm just tripping, man, 'cause I just wish that you would have put me down a lot sooner. We could have really helped one another."

"I don't think that the time was quite right, yet," Tony told him seriously. "I was still sort of unsure about what I was gonna do with all of this shit."

"Well, do you know what you're going to do, now?" Tommy asked.

"Yup..." Tony told him, "you and I, we're gonna start our own little army and really take over these streets together. Both of us eat on this block, and we both consider this our home. I don't know about you, kid, but I lay here... I die here."

Tommy though for a second, and then he nodded. His facial expression became serious. "Yo, I'm with you all the way, ya heard. I'll make a couple of calls... bring a couple of my realest goons through, and we'll screen them together, you know, figure out who's ready to take it to the next level."

Yeah, that's a bet. I'll gather my soldiers, as well. Ain't no need in wasting anymore time. It already looks as if the fucking world might be coming to an end," Tony said, his quip not that amusing, yet he hadn't quite intended for it to be.

"You ain't never lie…" Tommy began to say, but the sound of his cell phone ringing interrupted their conversation.

Holding up a hand to be excused, he stepped several feet outside of the room and took the call. In just a matter of seconds, without so much as a goodbye, he shot out of the office and headed for the front exit, running at full speed.

3

Curtis forced his way through the rapidly growing crowd of onlookers. Making it across the street, he finally reached a clearing on the sidewalk, but there was yellow crime scene tape keeping him a good bit of a distance away from the actual wreckage.

His heart raced as he stood staring at his terribly bashed in Mercedes. The authorities had somehow moved it so that it now faced in his direction, implicating that Lamont had been traveling down the sidewalk.

Klick Klak knew that that wasn't the case, though, because from the looks of the frontend of his car, his brother had more than likely ran into the siding of one of the many brick buildings. Anxiety nearly overcame him, as he began to wonder about Lamont's well-being.

Frantically, he searched for him until his weary eyes stopped on a lone paramedic truck. There were two ems workers loading a gurney inside of it, and Klick Klak tried not to panic at the sight of the sheet-covered still figure lying atop of it. He rushed his way over to them, but not without having to first wrestle his way through a couple of on-duty cops.

Pushing his way past them, he came to a halt at the rear of the truck and pleaded with the medics to allow him the opportunity to identify whoever the victim might be. Out of pure curiosity, they did so. Leaning inside, Klick Klak tugged at the bottom of the sheet, exposing the victims face. It was a young female. With a look of shock, he stepped back and glancing back down toward the scene of the accident, he asked, "Where's the driver of that car?" "Why... do you know this little girl?" one of the two male medics questioned.

"No, but that's my car over there," he spat irritably.

"So, are you aware of who was driving it?" he heard a voice ask from behind him. He turned and stared at a tall, potbellied, balding black cop who appeared to be chewing on something, but in all actuality, he was just outright toothless. The man's head craned toward the totaled vehicle. "Yes..." Klick Klak told him matter of fact, "it was my little brother."

Raising a hand, the cop gestured toward an idling squad car that sat several yards away. "Is that him?" he asked. "Awe, fuck no...come on man. What did he do?" Klick Klak asked, as he attempted to close the distance between where he stood, and his brother sat handcuffed inside of the back of the police vehicle. There was an anguished expression on his face.

"Wait a minute, son..." the cop said placing a firm hand on Klick Klak's shoulder. Gritting his teeth, Curtis had to fight the urge to smack the constantly gumming man's hand away. He stared at him with warning eyes. Unseeingly bothered, the cop stepped in closer to him so that only Klick Klak could hear his next words.

"Looks like we have ourselves here a dilemma. I'm assuming that that's really your little brother over there…"

Klick Klak said nothing. "Well, he's currently in a great deal of trouble. Seems to have gotten himself in a bit of a jam-killing that poor little girl, there, with his careless driving."

The toothless official paused while letting that bit of troubling news sink in. He shook his head staring pitifully into the ambulance's direction.

"Yeah, I can see that" Curtis spoke, his voice sounding weary. The older man continued. "He doesn't even look old enough to buy liquor, yet." He looked at Klick Klak waiting for an answer. When none came, he continued.

"Tell me… how often do you allow your brother to drive your car?"

"Whenever he wants to. Doesn't matter much to me, because I've got several vehicles. That's my little brother… I just about give him whenever he wants, just as he keeps his grades up in school?"

"Yeah," Curtis said matter-of-factly.

"And I assume that he's doing quite well?" the man asked.

"He was driving me Mercedes, wasn't he?" Klick Klak answered and growing annoyed he snatched his shoulder free of cop's grasp.

Without as much as a flinch, the cop continued.

"Now you see, I figured that… and that's what bothers me. You're telling me that he's doing well in school, yet I found this in his pocket when I searched him, before putting him in the backseat of that cruiser."

His other hand that had been resting at his side now sat palm up, and Klick Klak stared down at it. His eyes grew wide, and his facial expression became a scowl. Darting his eyes into his brother's direction was enough condemnation for Lamont to understand what the officer had shown him and caused the younger man to hang his head.

The cop began speaking again, demanding Curtis' attention.

"You know what this is, don't you?" "It looks like fucking heroin," Klick Klak said disgustedly, and trying to appear bewildered.

"You know where he might have gotten it from?" Klick Klak's jaw tightened.

"Nah…I don't have a clue," he told him, and that was the honest truth. He had no idea where Lamont had gotten the bundle of smack from, or who had been the person that sold it to him. He vowed to himself to find out, though, because someone was in serious trouble for selling his little brother some dope for resale.

"You don't sell this stuff, do you?" the cop asked skeptically.

"Hell nah…" Curtis said, although the cop didn't buy it. He knew Curtis better than he thought. "No Teeth looked around cautiously to make certain that no one had come into earshot. Satisfied, he turned back to face Klick Klak. "Listen, I ain't buying that shit, boy. I've been doing this here for the past thirty-two years of my life, and I've been watching young men like you right now, but you're in a position to help him out."

"What in the fuck do you mean?" Klick Klak asked, not caring to disguise his dislike for the cop anymore. "What I mean is that if I turn this here dope in, then your little schoolboy's freedom goes down the drain. And instead of being charged with an accidental death by motor vehicle, he'll go down for something more serious. It's obvious that he lost control of the car while driving, because he was more than likely trying to take a call… one that would have been about some form of drug transaction."

"You don't know that" Klick Klak spat.

"But the district attorney's office will make a damn good argument of it." Curtis grimaced.

"Hmm… that's what I thought," the coop boasted, obviously recognizing defeat when he saw it.

"I could make this go away," he said opening up his hand again for Klick Klak to see.

"What the hell do you want, man?" Curtis asked, cursing Lamont for his stupidity. He'd warned him…now look at what was happening to them. This was what the cop had been waiting for. "Just a measly five percent of what you make every month, for the next two years."

Curtis looked at the man's name and badge number just for assurance. There was not anyway that this bastard was going to get away with what he was trying to do. And although he was appalled, he'd play along, just to get his brother out of the rut that he was in. "That's a lot of extra cash for an old man," he said making an attempt at a slight jest. "About to retire…" the man said, "need the extra ends."

"Yeah, well, it'll be more than enough."

"So, we have a deal, then?"

"I guess the fuck so!" Klick Klak said no longer hiding his disgust, knowing that he was making a deal with the devil. He watched as the officer tucked the drugs back into his pants pocket.

Just then there was a loud ear-piercing shriek that came from some several yards away. Both of the men turned into the direction in which it had come from. Curtis eyes grew wide. "Shit," he said at the sight of the person standing not far from them, "what's he doing here?"

Tommy was glaring into the rear of the ambulance truck, wailing in pure anguish.

"Alaena!" he screamed.

4

Climbing from her vehicle, Stephanie hastily made her way over to Tommy's side. She immediately raised her hands and covered her mouth to conceal her own wails, as she stared into the back of the ambulance in disbelief.

Turning to her right, she reached out to console her lover, but it was too late. He was headed into the other direction. Straining her eyes, Stephanie tried hard to see where he was so determined to go off to, but the unrelenting rain prevented her from seeing anymore than several feet in front of her. Somewhere in the direction that Tommy had gone, there were some loud words exchanged, followed by a clashing sound. She thought she heard a barrage of profanities, before a little more than a dozen people ran off into that same direction. Then came the sound of someone tussling.

"No, Tommy!" Stephanie yelled, as she ran toward the crowd. "I'm gonna kill you, motherfucker!" Tommy yelled, as he tried with every bit of strength that he had in him to pull Lamont through the shattered rear-window of the police cruiser that he sat handcuffed inside of.

There were several police officers making an attempt to pull him away

Stephanie couldn't quite make out the identity of the person inside of the car but the voice of the man standing not too far from her caught her attention. She looked beside her, and that's when recollection kicked in.

"Get the fuck off of my brother!" Klick Klak growled in anger. She noticed that there were a group of gentlemen shielding him from proceeding any further, though, they were not the police. A surge of panic shook throughout her entire body like a violent case of tremors, and her legs threatened to give out. This can't be happening, she thought. Curtis' little brother can't have been the cause of Alaena's death. Tommy loves that little girl so much. There's no way that they're going to end this war, now.

Tears began to stream down her face, yet they went unnoticed because of the rain. "Tommy!" she called out to him, hoping desperately that she'd be able to gin his attention. "Tommy, baby, please…"

To Stephanie's relief, he broke free of the police officers' hold and staggered toward her. She held out her arms, and with every ounce of strength that she had in her, she held him tightly. With his head hung low over her shoulder, his body racked with sobs as the pain overtook him.

"Why, baby?" he cried into her hair. She said nothing, but she tried her best to soothe him. Stephanie watched as the group of men that held Curtis released him, and he trotted over to where his brother sat inside of the police cruiser.

It appeared that some words were exchanged between two of them, before Klick Klak turned and headed into their direction, the group of guys that had been restraining hi directly on his heels.

Stephanie now knew that they were his crew. Nearing them, Curtis stopped and called Tommy's name. The rain had picked up even more, and as if nature could sense the rippling anguish, the winds began to blow more harshly.

Tommy turned at the sound of the familiar voice and pure hatred shown in his eyes.

"What the fuck do you want?" he asked once he turned to face Curtis.

There was a breath between the two, before Klick Klak told him, "I'm sorry about your sister."

Without giving Curtis' words any thought, Tommy reared back and attempted to spit in his enemy's face. In that very instant, all hell broke loose.

5

Down at the police headquarters things had gotten pretty rile up by the time that both Tommy and Curtis had been booked for disorderly conduct. They were both being held in separate bullpens.

After briefly questioning several of the onlookers that had been present at the scene of the accident, it had become quite clear to the authorities who exactly these two young men were, and what had happened to the little girl, it was rejoicing to know that they'd finally found out who was responsible for flooding their already desecrated streets with heroin. The public abuse of the hideous drug was vastly becoming a problem, like some sort of an outbreak. There were zombies everywhere, infesting every alleyway and bridge underpass in town. If anything were determined to make it something positive, seeing as how the ending of her precious life was the start of their beautiful beginning. Cleaning up these streets was a must for some... a dream that their little police spirits yearned to come true. Whereas for an elite group of others, the grime that had overcome the city of Paterson was just what the doctor ordered.

When Officer Sims approached the cell that Klick Klak was being held in, he found the young black man lying face-up on the metallic bench that protruded from one of the mossy-green colored stone walls. His forearm was draped over his eyes, and he appeared to rest.

"Hey, dope boy..." the cop called as quietly as he could. There was hint of sarcasm in tone.

"What the fuck do you want?" Curtis asked, glancing up and seeing the toothless official from earlier. The baldheaded man chuckled. "We've had that discussion already, but...I figured that you'd like to know that your brother has already been released."

Klick Klak sat up straight.

"Word? Yo, don't be playin' with me, man."

"Word..." the man said more seriously, "but don't think that that means you can just gon' and forget about what we talked about. The district attorney just decided not to charge him...yet. Don't forget that I still have this here little sack of treats that I can bet my gums on has got his fingerprints all over it. Plus...and I hate to be the bearer of bad news..." he said while snickering. He cleared his throat and continued, "The entire department now knows that you and your archrival over there are the ones behind the sudden surge in heroin abuse."

"What the fuck you mean?" Curtis asked heatedly, jumping to his feet and swiftly approaching the bars. "You dirty motherfucker... you dropped a dime on me?"

"Calm yo black ass down, boy, before I come in there and kick you another shithole," the cop hissed through his toothless grill. "You ignorant little motherfucker, I didn't do a damn thing. You can thank some of those 'not-so-grateful' fans that y'all have accumulated throughout the city for that. You see, I might be old, but I'm about my paper. I know you out there getting' that fettuccini, nigga, and I want in. I got to eat, dope boy...and my retirement time is coming up. That pension shit ain't gone do nothing for the life that I'm trying to live. So now, you see, I need you and you are damn sure need me. I'll keep these motherfuckers ten steps behind you. You just give me what I asked for."

A couple of seconds passed before Klick Klak sighed and gave the eager official an assuring nod. He turned to walk back toward the bench, but the sound of keys and the gate unlocking stopped him in his tracks.

He turned and saw Officer Sims still standing there waiting.

"Oh, I forgot to tell you..." he said smiling, his pink gums on display, "you made bail."

Tommy was furious. Six hours had passed since he'd gotten out of jail, and he now stood back inside of Tony's barbershop, in the presence of his girlfriend and the most trusted of his crew, Tony included. He was pacing back and forth in front of the window, only stopping when, miraculously, a customer would appear, and he had to step out of their way so they could enter.

Stephanie sat in silence not far from him. She was trying her best not to stress over his current disposition, but couldn't help watching him with intensity. She too failed miserably at trying to calm her nerves. That form of peace, she knew, would be foreign to the both of them for a while. Her man, impetuous Tommy, wasn't one to let troublesome matters go so easily, especially one that involved the tragic death of one of his enemy's closest relatives. Stephanie was sure that the only thing that would diffuse this deadly quarrel was just that...more death.

Her stomach churned when she thought about the fact that that occurrence could lie on both sides of the field. She wasn't ready to lose Tommy. She loved him entirely too much to even dwell on the thought for any longer than necessary. He was her world; she'd be lost without him... dead inside.

"Tommy..." she called out to him, but he paid her no mind. He was mumbling something under his breath and wringing his hands with great agitation. The word 'kills' slipped from his lips, and that urged Stephanie to demand his attention without omission.

"Tommy!" she yelled, drawing everyone's gaze. She paid them no mind, as he turned sharply to face her.

Her had an angry expression on his face and looked as though he'd been snatched from a devilishly pleasant daydream.

"Come here…" she said calmly, patting the seat beside her, "and sit down."

Tommy paused for a second as if he were contemplating her request. With a sigh, he closed the distance between them and complied. He leaned forward and rested his elbows on his knees, running his hands frantically through his close-cropped hair. He nearly flinched when Stephanie placed a gentle hand on the back of his neck and began to knead the tenseness out of his muscles.

She leaned over kissed his temple. "You alright, baby?" she asked, already knowing the answer to her rhetorical question.

He shook his head with annoyance, still not speaking. She noticed that there were tiny little wet stains appearing on his previous dried denim jeans and realized that he was once again shedding tears.

Her heart aching badly for Tommy, she pulled him closer and cradled his head against her chest. "Please, baby, stop crying…" she pleaded with him. "It's breaking my heart, Tommy." Several tears escaped her own eyes, yet she bothered not to wipe them away.

A cell phone rang, and Tony's voice sliced through the room. "Yeah..." he answered, his deep tone sounding wary as well. He waited for a fraction of a second. "Word? When?"

Another pause, then, "Aiight...I appreciate it. Mmmm hmmm... I'll speak to you later. Take it easy, Trish...and thanks."

He hung up and looked over at Tommy from where he stood.

"Just found out that both of them are out of jail, not just Curtis." Tommy pulled away from Stephanie and his gaze shot to Tony. "What do you mean ... how are they both out of jail? That little motherfucker just killed my sis..."

"The D.A. didn't charge Lamont," Tony said, cutting him off. In a flash, Tommy stood, his chest heaving as he faced the shop's door. Somehow, he'd managed to pull the 40. Caliber pistol that he'd been carrying free in the process.

Breathing heavily, he cocked the weapon and stared out of the shop's front window as an unmarked patrol car went passing by. His chest rose up and down like a maddened gorilla, as he contemplated blasting on the government official.

6

The storm was progressing beyond belief. The winds had already grown to a howling pitch, and the rain not only pelted and soaked everything on the earth's surface and all that lie in between, but the hail that came along with it was alarmingly abusive. The two bedroom house that Curtis and Lamont shared near the outskirts of Paterson had been built to withstand natural disasters such as the one that was headed their way, but only time would tell whether or not the modern home would live up to the standards that the realtor had assured Curtis it would.

Outside, the scenery was one to remember; beautiful in its own way, but horrific to those that were prone to flinching at the slightest sound of thunder and lightning. Had there not been so much racket on the exterior of the Crowder's residence, passersby would have probably worried over the storm that was brewing inside of the home. It was a troublesome rave that could erupt into something more perilous at any time.

"Lamont, what the hell were you thinking...trying to push heroin?"

"What do mean, Curt? I was tryna do me, man... get my own money...like you do!"

"Say what…boy, are you stupid? You're a kid…not a dope boy!"

"Aye, yo, son, I'm a man! I can hold my own and get my own dough!"

"Little motherfucka, you ain't nothing but seventeen! You ain't even had time to grow hair on ya nuts, yet!" Curtis screamed.

"I ain't no damn kid, Curt… that's exactly where the fuck you've gotten it wrong! I can take care of myself!" Enraged by his brother's words, Klick Klak's fists balled at his side and his teeth grinded together.

"I mean, damn, look at what all I've seen growing up around you, bruh. Look at how I've been raised! You…"

"Aye, yo, shut the fuck up!" Curtis said cutting him off. "Don't try dropping that bullshit off on me. I've not subjected you to the lifestyle that I chose. Even though you knew, I've had the decency to keep the day to day hustle hidden from your eyes. I've been as discreet as I could have been and have never blatantly put that shit in your line of vision, so don't go trying to put that shit off on me like that."

Lamont sighed heavily and shook his head in agitation. He and Curtis stood several feet away from one another, and even though Klick Klak was the older of the two, visibly it didn't appear to be so, because of Lamont's football stature . Although, he knew that with Curtis, it wouldn't make much of a difference, because his brother was much more experienced when it came to physical confrontation than he.

"You don't understand…" Lamont tried telling him with frustration. "I don't understand what? Please, explain it to me, Lamont," Klick Klak growled.

"Man, I don't want all of this school shit that you're trying to put off on me. I ain't trying to go off and play in the NFL. That's what you want me to do .   Those are your dreams; they ain't mine."

"What the fuck do you mean?" Klick Klak asked. This was the first that he's ever heard of his brother's disapproval of the future that he had planned for him. "I thought that you wanted to go off to college, 'L'. I thought that you wanted to get up out of the 'hood… be somebody…somebody better than who the fuck I've become."

"I do …" Lamont assured him with determination, trying to get his brother to understand.

Curtis was confused. "Then why have you chosen to take the same path as I have?"

"See, that's just it… you aiight, bruh. You're doing good for yourself, and I can see that, eventually, you're gonna be able to get up out of the 'hood, anyhow…no matter how you had to do it. You've made it through the grime. Heroin got you all caked up. Why can't that be me? Why can't I do it like that, too?" Lamont asked pleadingly. "Cause, man… I want better for you. I don't want you to be like me!" Curtis told him seriously. "Damn, bruh...don't you get it? That's the point...I want to be just like you."

Lamont's confession caused him to stammer, and he had to take a step back to gather his thoughts. Curtis wondered how it had gotten to this, with all of the extreme measures that he'd taken to prevent it.

"Yo, Curt, I see all of the love that everybody shows you, and I admire that. People treat you like you're a fucking king, or something and I want that too," Lamont told him. His brother seemed to be considering his last words, and he hoped that Klick Klak was beginning to understand his way of thinking.

Abruptly, Curtis charged at him and yanked him up by the front of his shirt. He took Lamont by surprise, and a tinge of fear jolted the young man into an erect stance. There was a fire in his eyes that Lamont had never seen before, and it scared him.

"You listen to me, you little ignorant motherfucka! Do you realize what chasing this life just cost you? There's a little girl dead, now, and I'm certain that this shit had something to do with you losing control of the car and crashing into her! Am I right?"

Lamont shivered, and nodded. There was a lump forming at the back of his throat, and his eyes became misty.

"I was trying to...answer the phone when a customer called." "Shit..." Klick Klak said, and his jaw clenched in worry and anger. He watched as tears began to run down his little brother's face, and loosening his grip on Lamont's shirt, he drew him into an embrace.

"Damn it, Lamont…"

The pain and realization of what he'd done came crashing down on the young gentleman, and a bout of sobs caused his shoulders to heave. "Damn, man…shhh, little bruh, it's gonna be alright. Chill, man… be easy…". Klick Klak said trying to calm him, "I got you. You know I do…this shit is gone be aiight."

"Aye yo, I fucked up, Curtis. I fucked up really bad, god."

Curtis said nothing more, as he consoled his brother and thought regretfully about the things sure to come. They were inevitable. There was no getting around it. Because Tommy's sister was dead and had been killed by his younger brother, a war was sure to ensue. No matter the mistake that he made.

7

As if Mother Nature were bestowing a blessing upon Stephanie, the torrential rains and whirling winds had abruptly subsided to an unbelievably mild shower, and she'd taken the opportunity to go out on a whim and pay someone a visit that she believed Tommy would have never agreed to allow her to go and see, had she confided in him beforehand. By the way that he'd reacted to the news that Tony had delivered, she'd saw then that there would be no reasoning with him. Immediate intervention was the only way that she believed she would be able to save the love of her life from doing something stupid. Whether he forgave her or not, in the end, she knew that this was the best that she could do to save him from himself. Explaining her motives to Tommy would have been of naught because he would have taken it as though she were saying that he needed to be saved from someone else harming him. He wouldn't understand that if he was left to handle these matters on his own, he'd surely bring about his own self-destruction. That she couldn't allow, because, if he destroyed himself, then he was destroying her as well. He was everything that she loved and there was no way in hell that she was going to lose him.

So, as Stephanie drove, for the second time that day, she said a hail Mary for Tommy, though this time she said it aloud and with more vehemence.

As she prayed, the sun began to peek through the clouds, and she took it as a good sign.

In just a matter of minutes, she'd be reaching her destination, yet she had yet to come up with the proper solution for how she was going to introduce herself. She hoped that her presence would be well-received. If she were unwelcome, she didn't know if she'd be able to just climb back into her car, and return home to Tommy without having put forth an effort to find a peace median between her lover and his foes.

Was it reasonable to just sit back and let him handle this on his own under his own terms?

Am I doing the right thing? she wondered nervously as she got closer and closer to her point of no return.

Her thoughts of uncertainty didn't matter how much, now, because the moment that she pulled into the driveway of the cozy-looking, two bedroom house, the front door opened and a neatly groomed German boxer, followed by a beautiful little caramel-skinned girl sheltered from the weather in a bright yellow raincoat came bounding out toward her.

She couldn't possibly have been expecting me, could she? Stephanie wondered.

She gazed further beyond the child and her dog and for a fraction of a second, she held her breath, as the last of her fears came and past. Standing with her arms crossed, and leaning against the front doorjamb, was the woman that she'd come to see. She didn't look to be upset. In fact, she looked… welcoming. Maybe even a bit hesitant, as she herself was.

Thinking of what Tommy's reaction might be to this visit, Stephanie was just about to reconsider her actions and back out of the driveway when, as if she were able to read her unannounced visitor's mind, Curtis' baby's mother waved for her to come inside.

Tommy had taken advantage of the break in the inclement weather, and he and Tony now rode four soldiers deep-six including themselves in Tommy's 2010 Ford Explorer, headed into the direction of a highly drug infested neighborhood located on the Westside. North main was the closest that they could get to Curtis' territory, without anyone sending a warning call his way-a call that would alert the area's leader that there were outsiders on his grounds.

Tommy had a cousin that lived and got money in this area. And none to his liking, his cousin was moving no other than the work provided by Curtis. It was Curtis' dope that

Jacob cut, then bagged and distributed day in and day out. A very displeasing act that Tommy could not stand. It wasn't his cousins' fault he had been raised on the Westside. But what Tommy couldn't understand was why Jacob would choose to work these slum streets for an outsider, when he could be getting money with him...his family. It was only a matter of Jacob saying that he was willing and ready to get down with him, and without hesitation, the wheels would-be set-in motion. Hell, he'd even be willing to give him his own block. He had it like that-he could do that for Jacob. Surely Jacob wasn't eating as well as he could be with him and Tony, over on the Eastside.

As he neared his cousin's apartment, he thought about the turn of events that had taken place, shifting things from already troubling, to horrible. The death of his baby-sister was too damn heavy on his heart. It had given him a headache just trying to calm his nerves. Tommy knew that he had to be strong... he could show no signs of weakness; especially not in front of the elite hit squad of four that he and Tony had screened and chosen. They were four of the most ruthless hustlers that they had known for nearly all of their lives. Tony, being the oldest of the bunch, had actually watched the young gentlemen grow. He'd watched them transcend from boyhood, and abruptly turn into rigid men. Not only were they fearless, but they knew how to make a dollar. Something that, if they won this war, would turn out to be beneficial to their entire crew... the 'D-Pound Crew' when this was over and done with.

Not even those shit-faced, fake ass mobster politicians, Tony thought, as he readjusted his chrome. .45 caliber pistol that sat tucked away in his waistband.

Tommy saw the gesture and instinctively, he felt for his sidearm, as well. All four men sitting in the seats behind them were quiet: Talil, Kwalib, Shahid, and Rayshawn. Each gunman had their own thoughts as to what they had pledged to, that day. They'd been promised something that, undeniably, each young man wanted. What every other member of any organization wanted... a brotherhood. Each new member of the 'D-Pound Crew' had been raised by the streets. None had had the luxury of sharing their short childhoods with siblings. Now they had backbone. They had family... they had clan. Most of all, they had the beginning of what Tommy and Tony had called a militia. Shit was about to get real, and they were all ready for what was to come. Pulling up in front of Jacob's apartment building, both Tommy and Tony got out, and all four of the other men followed. They stepped up onto the porch, and Tommy rang the doorbell to the first-floor apartment.

In just a matter of seconds, the large steel door was being quickly unlocked and pulled open. Jacob stood before them with a sheepish grin. "What's really good, Tommy? It's good to see you, cousin, he said, extending his fist to give Tommy some dap. They pounded fists, and Jacob and Tony did the same. Taking an immediate notice of their grim facial expressions, he looked back to Tommy and became aware of what he hadn't paid any attention to before. His cousin bore the same exact expression as the other gentlemen. Cautiously, he asked,

"Yo, what's up…what's with the ill ass grills?"

Tommy willed himself to be patient. "Jake, I need to talk to you, man…it's urgent. Can I come in?" "Yeah…yeah, man, y'all come in," he said stepping aside, and allowing his cousin and his crew to enter.

Before shutting his apartment building's door back, though, he took a speculative look out into the street to see if anyone else had accompanied them as well as to make certain that none of the local hustlers saw this many of the 'DPC' members entering his crib. Everyone knew that he and Tommy were cousins, and that Tommy wanted badly for him to leave the Westside and go over to the East to get down with his team. Because of that public knowledge, Jacob had to be careful. He didn't want, nor need any of his boys getting the wrong idea about what his intentions were.

They waited patiently for him inside of the hallway, until he led them down the corridor to his door. Turning the knob and stepping inside, he hollered out to his girlfriend to let her know that they had company.

"Ieisha, girl, Tommy's here...come and say what's up!" Not having seen the sexy brown-skinned beauty in sometime, Tommy had forgotten how gorgeous his cousin's girlfriend was. Both he and Jacob having been raised in the 'hood, it was expected for at least one of them to date a black girl, but damn... who would have thought that his cousin would have gone out and gotten the finest one in Paterson. They had been together for four years, now, and it was obvious that they were in love.

Coming around the corner wearing one of Jacob's white tee-shirts, and a pair of fitting gray sweatpants, Ieisha beamed gleefully at Tommy, before she noticed his accompanying entourage.

"Hey, Tommy...what's up?"

He couldn't help but to smile down at the diva, as she hugged him. She was glowing, and he could tell that they were interrupting some of her and Jacob's private time. "Sorry to intrude..." he said releasing her. "It's alright," she said, walking over to where Jacob was standing, not disputing Tommy's assumptions, "we've got all day." She winked at Jake, and he grinned back at her. "Well, y'all have a seat," she said with a wave of her hand, and accepting the offer, every one of them found their own seating arrangements on one of the several couches inside of the spacious living room.

Comfortable where they were, both Jacob and Ieisha continued to stand with one another. Pain ripped through Tommy's core, as he took his time explaining the events that had taken place. He left out no details, nor did he fabricate what any of his intentions for his enemy would be while seeking retribution.

Jacob listened intently and fought hard not to give in to the wobbly feeling that he felt in his knees. By the time that Tommy had finished relaying the news to them, it seemed that Ieisha was now supporting his weight instead of he hers'. "Wait...wait..." Jacob stammered, "who did you say did this?" "I told you..." Tommy said agitatedly, "the little brother of that motherfucker that you be hustling for. It was that dumb ass wanna-be that hit Alaena." He spat his last words out so ferociously that it made Ieisha cower and tuck her face in Jacob's shoulder.

"Fuck..." Jacob said, forcing himself to study the faces of the rest of the men more thoroughly, now. He needed to find out whether or not if they all felt the same way about his trapping cronies as his cousin did. He didn't want any of them to get it misconstrued-he was deeply sorry about the death of his cousin's sister, because she too was his family, but he had to be realistic about the issue. All of his life he'd lived on this side of town, and had grown up around Curtis, alongside all of the other hustlers that they got money with. He had love for 'One-Two Live'…his entourage…the entourage. Everybody from Paterson, to Newark knew that that was the hardest and most thorough click around. Everyone else was just a shadow compared to what they were. There was no way Jacob could turn on the only brothers that he knew. And as he stared into his cousin's eyes, he hoped feverishly that Tommy would reconsider. Especially since he'd been the one that had sold Curtis' little brother the bundle of heroin that he'd been riding around distributing when he'd lost control of the car and had run into Alaena.

If Tommy meant for an all-out war against 'One-Two Live', then he meant war against Jacob as well. Unless Jake was going to join them. It hit Jacob then and there. Full of sorrow, he now understood. He was about to break his cousin's heart beyond repair, and undoubtedly their familial bond would be forever severed.

"Ieisha…" Jake said looking down at her, and gently kissing the top of her head. "Hmm?" she asked, her face still buried inside of his shoulder. "Go and wait for me inside of the bedroom while I finish talking to Tommy and his crew." "Okay," she said sniffling, and that's when he realized that she'd been crying. Before turning to leave she stole a glance at

Tommy, and through their eye contact he accepted her condolences.

Once Jacob heard their bedroom door click shut, he turned and faced Tommy and his crew. Standing firm, he spoke once again. "I know why you're here, cousin…and I can't…"

Several seconds of silence passed between the two of them, before Tommy stood.

"What do you mean you can't?" "I can't, yo. You…you want me to turn against my click, and ride with you against 'One-Two Live', but Tommy I fuck with Klick Klak and the rest of them cats. I grew up with them." "What the fuck do you mean?" Tommy growled. "One of them bitches killed my sister… your cousin, and you ain't down?"

"I can't!" Jacob nearly yelled at him. "Why the fuck not?" "Because what?" Tommy questioned on the verge of losing total control. The rise and fall of his chest became rapid, as his breathing picked up and came in short gasps of air. He was a lion in a gorilla's stance, ready to pounce on anyone in opposition to him and tear them apart. "Because I'm the one who supplies Klick Klak's little brother, Lamont!" Jacob hissed without as much as a hint of hesitation in his confession.

Silence followed and the faint sound of rustling clothes pierced through the quiet room, as Tony and the four other 'DPC' members stood. Then it happened. Tommy lunged, and something metallic came down hard across

Jacob's face. He staggered to his left, but someone was there, too, waiting for him, and they caught him again.

Fists and pistols rained down on him, as he lay balled into a fetal position, trying with everything that he had in him to protect himself from anymore head trauma. The attempt was useless, though, as they pulled on his limbs and continued to assault him with as much brutal force as they could muster.

Jacob's world became a blur. In just a matter of minutes, he'd gone from making healthy love to his girl, to being so badly beaten that he no longer felt any pain. He didn't even know if any of his limbs still worked nor did he even care to try to find out. Only one thing mattered to him at that point and it wasn't what anyone would have thought it would be, which was Ieisha's safety.   No, that's not what clouded his thoughts, as he drifted off into a place of peace. It was the face... the face. The face of a beautiful little girl as she glared lovingly at him. She seemed so happy, and she appeared to be safe wherever she was. There seemed to be something surrounding her... something bright-,like a big fluffy cloud. The cloud shifted, then separated, and turned into a large group of people clothed in white...bright white.

Alaena smiled, and Jacob's breath caught. Just as he was about to apologize to her for what had happened, an ear-piercing shriek ripped its way through his final reunion with his now   deceased   cousin.   He   immediately recognized the voice.

"Stop!" Ieshia screamed, as she ran from their bedroom and launched herself at Tommy's back. The sight of her being pushed across the floor was the last thing that Jacob remembered seeing, before his vison faded to blackness.

8

By now, the rain had come to an official halt. Overhead, the clouds were thick in the sky, giving the earth's surface a grayish look, yet you could see the sun trying to force its way through the condensed mass of particles that harbored the destructive waters that had previously been battering the planet's surface, and everything in between.

At present, the luminous ball of fire seemed like a savior to many. With all that had abruptly transpired, it seemed as if the rain had brought much tragedy along with it. Not only was there an uncomfortable amount of humidity in the air-irritating beyond measure, but there was also a heightened level of intensity that was seemingly growing by the hour.

There were an increasing number of pedestrians strolling about, but no one seemed to be entirely convinced that the storm was over just yet. They walked about, to and from their locations on high alert. Their umbrellas tucked safely at their sides, waiting for the next sign of a downpour to return.

No one paused in the same spot for any longer than they had to. There was no fraternizing, no corner-hanging, no 'hey, how you are doing... would you like to grab something to eat?' No, there was none of that. Everyone seemed to be on their own little excursions, the next person just an unwanted obstacle in their path.

As Klick Klak drove, he took notice of it all. The way that a young couple hunkered together, as they strolled down the sidewalk, the male of the two protectively cradling his partner with the intention of sheltering her from any natural dangers. The way that a mother held on tightly to her child, as she waited impatiently for a transit bus to arrive. He noticed how an elderly couple shuffled up the street, unable to pull their gazes from the disturbing skies. It was, in itself, a frightening sight to see. As if cordiality had suddenly ceased to exist.

Klick Klak was in a deep contemplation, as the rain-soaked highway passed beneath him. He was only several minutes away from reaching Denise's house;[1]his daughter's mother and girlfriend for the past eight years. There had once been a time when he and Denise had lived together under the same roof, but because of his lifestyle, he'd had to make the decision to live separately from her, once she'd learned what he had intended to do she'd been hysterical believing that he'd been trying to slowly distance himself from her. But in the end, after convincing her that it was entirely for her and their daughter's safety, she'd been more cooperative and willing to comply. And just as they'd hoped for, it had all worked out. Their living under separate roofs had actually been the quirk in their relationship that had helped them survive some of the worst of trials throughout their eight years together. They never seemed to tire of one another.

To Curtis's crew, he and Neesy were the dynamic duo. She was the hot to his cold, the sun to his moon, the fire to his water, and the yang to his yin. Denise knew her man through and through. She knew what he hated, and she knew exactly what he loved. She was highly aware of the things that bothered and angered him, and what made him smile. She knew what pleased and displeased her man. There wasn't much about Curtis that Neesy wasn't aware of. Even at times when he wouldn't speak verbally with her about his troubles, she would still somehow know what was wrong. Because of the loving trait that she possessed; he'd begun looking at her as the peace to his never-ending storm; a storm that never seemed to die out. A storm that, some way or another, Denise always seemed to be able to weather, even when he felt like giving up.

So, as always, forced to undergo the situation that he was now in, he was seeking out her love and serenity to help navigate his coming turmoil; a voyage that would no doubt lead to more pain, before it did solace.

Rounding the corner to her two-bedroom townhouse on Elmwood Drive, he caught sight of an unfamiliar vehicle sitting in Denise's driveway. It wasn't like her to have many visitors, so he wondered who in fact the person might be. Denise had quite a bit of family in Paterson, but none of them drove a money-green 2010 Dodge Challenger with twenty-four-inch custom chrome rims on it. Never having seen the car before, he grew suspicious and checked his hip for his piece. Flipping off the safety, he felt a little more secure knowing that it was there and ready if he just so happened to need it.

Climbing out of his car, Curtis made his way up to the front door. He listened carefully, before he slid his key inside of the lock and granted himself entry. Inside the spacious living room, it was quiet, which wasn't out of the ordinary for Denise. Glancing around at the homey quarters, Curtis couldn't help but to relax. He loved coming over to his woman's house, because it always made him feel so… at home, and safe. The smells, the soft furniture, and the paintings that hung perfectly from the walls just added to the euphoric feeling that he always got, whenever he was in Denise's presence. It all played on his senses like a sweet melody being strummed by a harpist. She and their daughter were truly his calm, and right now he had to find them.

He sighed and made his way upstairs. Still, there was nothing but silence that surrounded him. When he made it to the top of the steps, he took a right down the carpeted hallway and passed by the bathroom. Taking a quick glance inside told him that no one was in there. He kept on until he reached his daughter's room, which was located on the left. The door was shut. Quietly letting himself inside, he shook his head in disappointment. Shakira's bed was fully made, and empty. Shutting the door back, he turned back down the hall and in a couple of strides made it to Denise's room…their room.

The door was slightly ajar, so he gave it a nudge and stepped inside. Empty. "Damn…" he said to himself, growing impatient, "where are you, woman?"

Just then, he heard a dog bark and noticed that one of the bedroom windows was open. It was the window that overlooked the backyard. He strained his ears to listen more intently and thought that he heard Shakira giggle playfully.

Crossing the room, he made his way over to the windows; its' sheer teal-green curtains flailing gently against the pane. Both the heat coming from the outdoors, and the bedroom's ceiling fan accompanied by the home's central air/heating unit sent chills crawling up Curtis' back. There was something unusual going on, and he could sense it.

Peering out of the window, he allowed his eyes to roam through the thirty-yard stretch of scattered elms and flowerbeds that had been planted to increase the value of the property. The thick gray clouds and their yellowish background gave the grounds an appearance that any professional photographer would have loved to capture.

Not too far out from the house, he spotted his daughter running in circles, as their dog Tyson playfully gave chase to her. His tongue lolled, and the little muscle-bound meatball seemed to be enjoying their game. To the right of them, he saw Denise. She was sitting on a bench with her back to him. Her vibrant hair hung loosely down the center of her back. He took notice of her posture and immediately noticed how tensely she sat. She appeared a bit uncomfortable. He watched as she ran a hand through her hair, and let it drop agitatedly back into her lap, as if she were annoyed by something. Her head moved from one side, and then to the other. Then she raised her hand and pointed at something, her neck rolling in that way that it does when a woman is telling someone off.

He figured it out then...she was talking to someone, but to whom he had no clue. Curtis' eyes searched past her. He thought that he saw someone...a head... a little girl's head. Leaning even further out of the window, he raised himself up on his toes, and craned his neck. No, it wasn't a little girl's head. It was a full-grown woman... a white woman... with long black, silky hair.

"Hey!" he yelled out as loudly as he could, and it startled both of the women. Curtis daughter stopped running from Tyson, and he leapt onto her, tackling her to the ground. Denise swiveled around sharply and strained her eyes so that she could see him. Then the other woman stood, glaring up at him as if he were the intruder.

Stephanie dusted off the seat of her jeans, and then crossed her arms protectively over her chest. "What in the fuck is she doing here?" Klick Klak said, as he stared down at his enemy's other half.

Back at the home that he and his brother shared together, Lamont was rummaging through his bedroom closet when his cell phone rang. Unconsciously reaching into his front right pocket where he normally kept it, he felt emptiness and realized that he'd left it on top of his dresser. Momentarily disregarding what he'd been in search of, he stood and crossed the room to retrieve his phone. Without bothering to view who the caller was, he answered.

"Yo..."

There was silence.

"Yo...hello?"

"Yo? Is that how you answer your phone, boy?" an unfamiliar voice asked.

"Man, what...who the fuck is this?" Lamont asked impatiently. There was a deep chuckle, before the caller answered. "Calm down, boy... you'll find out who this is in due time. First, though, let me tell you who you are."

"Aye, man, who the fuck is this?"

"Shut the fuck up, boy, and listen to me!" the caller yelled, cutting Lamont's nervous ranting short. When there was complete silence, other than the sound of Lamont's regulated breathing there was that same deep chuckle on the other end.

"Now…as I was saying, you are the little piece of shit whose ass I just saved today. Yes, that's right…or else you would have been in a whole lot more trouble then what you are in now."

"Who are you?" Lamont asked trying to sound calm.

"Lose something, today?" the voice asked.

"What do you mean… did I lose something? Like what?"

"Little brown package…clear vials…black tar?"

The caller could hear the lump in Lamont's throat, as he forced himself to swallow. "Hmm…" the voice said, "that's exactly what I was thinking, you know, this is not what I expected from you. A little more gratitude would be greatly appreciated. I did save your little piece-of-shit ass from a felony murder charge."

"What do you want?" Lamont asked stiffly. He didn't know exactly which one it was, but it didn't take a rocket scientist to figure out that his surprise telephone stalker was one of the police officers that had been at the scene of the accident. Thinking back, he realized that he had been so far out of it all the time that he couldn't even remember which one of them it was that had searched him, or any of the alien faces that had been there. At present, they were nothing more than a blur to him.

This time the voice gave a hefty laugh. "What I want, boy, I'm quite sure that your little penny-pinching ass couldn't give me. You're smalltime, not a big-league player. You don't make enough money for what I've got in mind. But guess what, little one... your big brother does. And he already knows what I want. So, don't you worry your little skinny pants off, because he's going to take care of me."

"Oh, yeah...then what in the fuck are you calling me for?" "Because you little motherfucker..." the voice growled at him angrily," I want to make sure that you don't fuck up anything else by getting in the way of things."

Lamont couldn't take it any longer. The caller's anonymity was really getting to him.

Man fuck you!" he screamed into his phone's receiver. "Fuck you! Fuck you! Fuck you! You can suck my...."

Click.

Breathing heavily, and trying badly to calm himself, he stared down at the phone as though it had grown a human head, a mixture of anger, confusion, utter perplexity, and fright overwhelming him.

"Fuck you!" Lamont spat one last time for good measure. He was about to head back over to finish up what he had been doing before the disturbing call, when his phone rang once more, startling him.

"Hello…" he snarled in agitation. The voice that spoke back to him sounded femininely timid, but sweet.

"Hello…who's this?"

"Yo, you called my phone," Lamont snapped. "Who's this?" The lady on the other end cleared her throat before she spoke "my name's Ieisha. I saw this number in my man's phone and didn't know who it belonged to. Thinking that the woman on the other end was no more than one of his homeboy's baby's mothers, he told her, "Aye, yo, look shorty, if you and your man are having some type of relationship problems, then you called the wrong phone, because I ain't no marriage counselor and I damn sure ain't no bitch that he's fuckin'. "Listen, I didn't say all of that, now did I? I just need to know why my man called you last?" Ieshia asked, still fighting the urge to give in to her impatience. "Look, ma, what's your boyfriend's name?" "Jacob…" she said, hoping that the name sounded familiar to him. "Jacob? Who are you talking about, Jake Boogey?"

Ieshia cringed at the sound of the alias that had been given to her boyfriend, because she hated that name.

"Yes…that's him," she said calmly.

Lamont became skeptical about her motives for calling and wondered about the woman's intentions.

"Yeah, shorty, that's my dude."

"So, why'd he call you?"

"Hold the fuck up-why? What's up with all of the twenty-one questions?"

"Because, I need to know, sir. That's why."

"Aye, look, woman, find your man and ask him, aiight!"

He was about to hang up when she began to plead.

"No, wait, please…I can't…"

She began to cry, and Lamont immediately became sympathetic.

"Damn, lady, what's wrong? Why can't you just ask him? That's your man- he should be able to tell you those things…not me." "Because…" she bellowed through the receiver, "he can't talk… he's in a coma." "A coma…what…what do you mean he's in a coma? What happened?" he asked shocked.

"They beat him…" she cried. "They nearly beat him to death!" "Who?" Lamont yelled at her, a terrible case of goosebumps rising all over his flesh. "His cousin, Tommy, and some…some of his boys from his crew." "Shit…Shit! Shit! Shit! Shit! Shit!" Lamont exclaimed, as fright set in for the third time that day.

Somehow, Jacob's cousin, Tommy, who ran the 'D-Pound Crew', had found out that Jake had been the one supplying him, and they'd gone and made an example out of Jake for betraying their family.

That had to be the reason why they assaulted him Lamont thought, as he paced nervously back and forth across his room's floor.

He hadn't thought that selling a little heroin would cause this much trouble.

When Curtis found out, he was going to be pissed. Jake was his man. He had grown silent, and Ieisha was done being patient with him. "Your name…what's your damn name? Why did Jake call you?"

Lamont was beyond scared. He wanted to tell her…confirm to the strange woman that her boyfriend had in fact called him last, but he couldn't and wouldn't tell her that he was Curtis' younger brother, and that Jake had called him to make certain that he'd been satisfied with the product that he had sold him.

"My name…my name is… he called because…" There was an immediate mute sound that followed, and Lamont stared down at the phone clueless as to why the woman had just hung up on him, that is until he saw that he was actually the one that had ended the call.

Looking around nervously, he knew what it was that he had to do. He had to get out of that house, and fast…before Curtis came home and found out what had happened to Jake Boogey.

9

By the time that Tommy and his crew made it back to Tony's shop, the place had gone from unbearably desolate, to jam-packed. Through the large glass windows, they could see that every chair inside was taken. Not unsurprisingly, there was a generous amount of customers waiting to be serviced.

The break in the weather had apparently brought those who had taken shelter out of hiding. They were all on an emergency run to their preferred stylist, just in case the weather that was predicted to return didn't let up again for some time. Tommy's four henchmen remained outside with the hired pushers, while he and Tony went inside. The intensity on both men's face shown clearly, as they passed by the shop's occupants without giving them so much as a glance.

Knowing Tony all too well, the barbers that rented chairs from him knew when he was pissed about something, so they let him be and continued to commerce amongst one another and their clients. Entering Tony's office several steps behind him, Tommy slammed the door shut with enough force to rattle the walls. They walked over to a small wet bar that Tony had designed himself, and Tommy found a seat on a high stool, while Tony made his way behind it.

The older of the two began to fix them a drink, as they gathered their thoughts in silence. While one was angered and undoubtedly ready for war, the other was   distressed and confused.

Tony wanted to physically eliminate someone. Tommy needed to figure out the depth of the actions that he'd just taken. He'd nearly killed his own cousin. He fought within himself-the demons that his body hosted trying hard to convince him that Jacob's beating had been justified.

But had it really been Jacobs fault? He wondered had the drugs that he'd sold Curtis' little brother really been the cause of that terrible accident. My sister died because of whatever mistake had been made. Somebody had to pay. Coming to the conclusion that what had been done had indeed been justified, he wasn't all that sure that retribution should have begun with his cousin. Even so, he couldn't understand why Jacob would choose his neighborhood over his family. In his eyes flesh and blood always came first, because flesh and blood would be their when no one else would. At least they were supposed to be. But Jacob had chosen his 'hood…so that was how it was going to be.

"We should've finished him off," Tony said breaking the silence. "And the girl, too." Tommy looked at him with a frown. "Nah, it was just a message…we sent a message. That was all that needed to be done. We let them motherfuckers know that I ain't playing."

"I'm just sayin', kid, what if that bitch puts the jakes on us? She saw all of our faces, yo," Tony said firmly. "She ain't stupid." "You sure?" Tommy just stared at him over the glass of Patron that he nursed. With as much patience as possible, he waited for his friend's paranoia to past. Tony sighed. "Okay, so there wasn't any real reason to body them, but what do we do when that shit gets back to Klick Klak?"

A disturbing look crossed Tommy's face, and it unnerved Tony. "That's exactly what the fuck I'm hoping for." Tommy saw Tony's look of uncertainty and became suspicious. "What…are you having second thoughts, or something?" he asked. Tony shook his head quickly. "Nah, it's just that if we're gonna start a war with these dudes, then we should have just gone ahead and eliminated one of them while we had the chance." Tommy thought deeply about what Tony had just said, and if he admitted it to himself, the man was right. 'One-Two Live' was the deepest click from Paterson, all the way to Jersey City. Going to war with them would be like the biblical warrior Jehoshaphat going into battle against an army of a thousand, with only three hundred soldiers of his own. If they didn't start knocking them off now, then it would be a suicide mission; a suicide mission that Tommy was willing to commit? Maybe…but initiating the war by murdering his flesh and blood? Now, that just wasn't something that he could live with. "That was my cousin…" Tommy said sternly. "Who was probably the cause of Alaena's death," Tony argued. "Hey!" Tommy warned. "I'm just saying…" Tony said knowing that he'd overstepped his boundaries. "Don't you speak of my sister!" Tommy yelled at him. He looked around both hatefully and frantically, as if someone else were in the room with them. "I don't want my sister's name coming out of anybody else's mouth that didn't know her like that." "Aiight, kid, chill…" Tony said apologetically, "I just don't want the team taking any losses if we gone do this." Tommy tried to calm himself, but his mood wouldn't allow him to. A couple of seconds of silence passed before he spoke again, and his voice was calm when he did so. "Yo, you know they're coming, right?"

Yeah, I know… and that's why I'm stressing," Tony told him. He stole a glance at the section of the wall that he knew his clandestine arsenal sat sheltered behind. 'We'll be ready, though." They locked eyes, then, and Tommy nodded. There was an urgent knock at the door, and Tony yelled for whoever it was to come in. Kwalib stepped inside of the office, his dark six-foot three frame appearing aggressive against the room's stark white.

"Aye, yo, Tommy and Tone, we've got a problem." His voice was deep and sliced through the air like an unwanted intrusion…as if this was the wrong place, and wrong time. Simultaneously, they both asked, "What's up?" "Somebody just merked one of the runners."

"What?" Tommy asked coming to a stand. "What the fuck...when?" "Just now, god." There was a loud crash in the background, followed by a barrage of screams. Both Tommy and Tony rushed toward the door where Kwalib stood and kept on past him. They made it to the front of the shop and saw what all of the commotion was about. There was a large Louisville Slugger lying in the middle of the floor with a sheet of torn paper attached to it. Thousands of glass particles surrounded it and were scattered everywhere. It was apparent that someone had thrown it through the front window, which was now nonexistent. Other than the crunching of his shoes as he walked over the shattered mixture of silicates, there was a hushed silence as Tony made his way over and picked up the bat. He snatched the note from it and read. One way or another, you're going to get off of this block, boy!

Tony's body heat temperature rose three degrees. There was a dull pain at the back of his skull that signified a major headache coming on. Behind him, he heard Tommy's footsteps as he crunched forward. He stopped in front of the broken window, and pointed across the street, where people were beginning to gather. "Look..." Tony followed Tommy's gaze, and then he saw it... saw what Kwalib had come to tell them. There, lying motionless on the pavement was a fifteen-year-old kid who'd been bludgeoned to death.

10

Stephanie's nerves were shot as she watched Klick Klak approach them. There was an expression on his face that told her he wasn't too happy about her being there, which was understandable seeing as how he was at war with the man in her life. She really hoped that once he heard her side of things, he'd be receptive to her intentions, and would be willing to put forth the effort to make things at least a little better between himself and Tommy.

She'd heard the sincerity in his voice when he'd given Tommy his condolences and was quite upset about the way that Tommy had reacted, although, she'd kept those feelings to herself. It was a very tragic ordeal, losing Alaena the way that they had, but the truth of the matter was that it was an accident. No matter whose fault it was. The precious little girl's death was unintentional, and if these men didn't get past their differences, then the next death that was sure to occur wouldn't be an accident. It would be in cold blood.

Stephanie didn't know how much more of this feuding she could stand. It was becoming too stressful for her to bear. Klick Klak reached them, and Denise stood to embrace him.

"Hey, baby…" she said wrapping her arms around him, while planting a kiss on his lips. "Hey, mami, what's up?" He patted her on her backside, before letting her go. "I see you've got company." It was a statement, more than it was a question. Turning back to face Stephanie who'd gotten up from the spot in the soft grass that she'd been sitting in, she said,

"Curtis, baby, this is Stephanie.She came to speak with us." Once again, his face shown with intensity. "Yeah, Neesy, I know who she is." Hesitantly, Stephanie walked toward him with her hand extended. There was a pause, but Klick Klak accepted the greeting. Unconsciously, he took note of her Sicilian beauty, and how fragile she seemed. Her hand felt smooth in his palm, yet she held a firm grip. Whatever her reason for being here, he could see that she was determined. As he'd done with Tommy, Klick Klak offered his sympathies. "I am very sorry about the loss of the little girl, and I mean that." Stephanie sighed, and she released his hand.

"I know, Curtis, and that is why I am here. I know that my fiance can be very bullheaded at times, but I can assure you that he's not really that bad of a person."

Klick Klak nodded. "He's just terribly hurt by the loss of his little sister," she told him. "And the fact that his rival's little brother was the cause of her death only makes it worse," he finished for her. "It pains me to admit it, Curtis, but yes that's right." "Daddy! Daddy! Daddy!" they all heard Shakira calling gleefully, as she bounced over to greet him with Tyson on her heels. Kneeling, he scooped her up into his arms and nestled her against his chest.

"Hey, baby-girl!" he said happily. Tyson danced around them playfully, so Klick Klak reached out and patted him on the head a couple of times. Touched by the show of affection, Stephanie waited. "Alright…" Denise said breaking up the reunion, and reaching out for Shakira, "come on, you…let's go inside and get you cleaned up, while your father and this nice lady talk." She glanced at Stephanie with one last warning glare.

Knowing that there would be some sort of snack waiting inside for her, Shakira complied without protest.

Both Klick Klak and Stephanie watched mother and daughter as they departed. "You have a beautiful family," she said drawing his attention back towards her. "Please…sit," he said gesturing toward the bench beside them. His cell phone began to ring, but he ignored it.

He took a seat not far from her, turning so that he could keep an eye on the wooded area behind them. Stephanie remained facing the clearing that Shakira and her dog had been playing in.

She continued,

"Curtis, the reason why I am here is because I am trying desperately to find a solution for you and Tommy."

Without looking at her, he asked,

"Now, why would you do that? It's your man's war... not yours. The women in our corners never get involved with this side of things, so why are you doing so?"

"Because, Curtis, I know what you and Tommy have been going through, and I don't want anyone else to get hurt. The both of you have your differences, but the both of you are internally one and the same."

"What...how do you figure that?" he asked curiously.

"Because all the both of you want to do is run your empires, get rich, and take care of your families," she told him.

He huffed, and declared, "Yeah, but every time I turn around my click is having to go and retaliate because of some bullshit that your man did or some of his people."

"So, when does it stop?" she asked sounding disgusted.

"After what happened today, I guess when one of us ceases to exist."

"No, that is not true," she told him with impatience. "Even then someone else will take whosever's place it is that needs to be taken, and they'll just pick up from where their successor left off."

"So, what? What do you think we should do, then? Just quit getting money?" he asked annoyed. "That's not gonna happen, cause even if both of us retire to separate fuckin' islands somewhere, then as you said someone will just pick up where we left off. Trust me, I learned that today. Someone's always waiting in the shadows to be just like one of us. And it's always someone close to you that'll want to take on your positives and negatives as their own... like your disputes with enemies." "So, do you consider Tommy one of your enemies?"

That question warranted a venomous stare, yet she didn't appear shaken by the way that he looked at her.

"Do you?" she asked.

"What do you think?"

Stephanie didn't respond.

"Your man wants me dead, and you ask me a fuckin' question like that."

"You know, the both of you are obnoxious, selfish, and vain. Neither of you realize the depth of the pain that your causing the people closest to you, because you're too stuck on filling your pockets."

"Aye, look, lady, you can refrain from all of the insults, 'because that won't get anywhere with me," he warned her. "They weren't insults, they were the truth and you know it," she told him.

"Listen, man, tell me why you're here, so we can get on with this, because I'm a busy man and I've got things that I need to take care of," he said sternly. He was growing weary of her presence, so he turned and faced the woods once again.

Stephanie took a deep breath and let it out.

"Curtis, I'm not saying this because I think it'll benefit me financially in the end, so please don't misunderstand me. But, I think that, if you and Tommy were to join forces and run the city of Paterson together, then all of this would die out eventually, and everyone will be happy with the position that they'll be in."

"And how in the hell do you suggest we do that?" he asked.

"Well, first… as a show of willingness to work with him, you'll have to raise the cost of your product to equal Tommy's, so that it can even out things. Both playing fields would be equivalent to one another. No one side would feel cheated while the other is getting richer," she said, relaying her theory to him. "What …hell no!" he told her hysterically, sounding offended by her suggestion. "I'm not raising my fucking products prices for anyone!"

"Curtis, wait…please, listen," she pleaded, and waited for him to calm down, before she spoke again.

"I can promise you that you'll not lose any of your fortune."

"Oh, I know that I damn well won't, because I'm not doing it," he told her.

The look that she gave him revealed her disapproval of his current attitude toward her idea. When Stephanie spoke again, she sounded defeated.

"I was only trying to help."

Her tone brought Klick Klak's eyes back to her face.

"Shit..." he swore, and shook his head, "I can't believe this."

He glared at her skeptically.

"And what if it doesn't work?"

Behind her eyes, he could see that a flint of hope had returned.

"I swear, Curtis, that if you'll give it a try, then I'll take care of the rest."

He swore again, then returned his gaze back to the woods. His cell phone began to ring again, and this time he withdrew it. He didn't recognize the number, so he didn't bother to answer it. "Thirty days..." he told Stephanie with authority. "I'll give your plan a try for thirty days, but if this shit doesn't work..."

There was a warning in his tone, and she heard it very clearly. "Thank you, Curtis," she said with a sigh.

"Don't thank me..." he told her staring deeply into the woods at something that had drawn his attention. He'd thought that he'd seen someone out there, moving in between the trees. "Just do your part."

"I will," she said standing, and holding out her hand to him.

This time he accepted it with a bit more firmness and held her hand longer than necessary.

"If this causes any more bloodshed on my crew's behalf, then their blood will be on your hands."

"I understand," she told him, and was relieved when he granted her release. She was just about to leave, when saw something to the left of them.

Startled, Stephanie pointed in that direction.

"Curtis...who's that?"

Turning, Curtis became rigid and his fingers twitched, as he contemplated reaching for his sidearm.

Standing about fifty yards out, was a tall black, baldheaded man in a gray suit glaring at them. He was watching them as if they were the intruders, and not him. He waved, but neither Curtis nor Stephanie waved back.

He smiled, and that's when Stephanie realized that the man in the wooded area didn't have any teeth.

11

The roads had dried up considerably, and more of Paterson's citizens began to move out and about. The sun was beginning to show itself more and more, as the day went on and the confidence levels of both commuters and pedestrians had returned.

Traffic flowed freely, as Lamont made his way up Route 80, pushing just over seventy miles per hour in Curtis' 2010 Dodge Charger SXT. He was headed to the place that had been a refuge for both he and his brother when they were children. Somewhere that he knew he'd be able to find some reprieve from his troubles.

It took approximately forty-five minutes to reach 540 Hollis Avenue in Queens, New York. Glaring at the house that he sat parked in front of, a warm sense of security swept over him. He remembered the adolescent years that he and Curtis had shared inside of the home. Being raised up under a roof with six other children had been difficult to adapt to at first, but in the end, it had proven to be a comforting experience. Because they had had so many brothers and sisters, they were never alone. When things had gotten difficult for one of them, there was always someone in the same age bracket that would be able to understand whatever they were going through, no matter their different races. Lamont being the problematic child that he was had been in constant need of someone's understanding. Especially since their caretaker had always been out working so that they'd be properly provided for, and Curtis being the eldest of the bunch, always having been consumed by the street life.

Curtis and Lamont had been the only two that were blood related, and they'd also been the last two to join the bunch. At very young ages they'd been orphaned and tossed into foster care. Lamont had known that it had been a stroke of luck that they'd landed a loving and caring foster parent, such as Sylvia Ortiz.

Throughout the years that they had spent under her roof, she had remained a single parent, devoted whole-heartedly to tending to her flock. Other than her job as a housekeeper for a wealthy family over in Manhattan, she'd never let anything get in between them. She'd loved them all as if they were her own. Until that disdainful day had come when Mommy Sylvia had come home early from work and found Curtis sitting at her dining room table, cutting, and bagging up a brick of heroin. The sight of her eldest son doing such a thing had broken her heart and had disgusted her deeply. She'd been torn, unable to stand the sight of him any longer. She had raised them all better than that-had never set a bad example for any of them. Yet, her most trusted had chosen the life of the devil.

Because of Curtis' actions, he'd been forced to move out of her home. She'd refused to let him taint the rest of her children with his evil, but he hadn't left alone. He'd taken Lamont along with him.

It had been years since he'd last seen Mommy Sylvia-her beautiful rotund face, and its undying glow. She was a stout little Hispanic woman of Cuban descent, standing at five foot three. She loved fitting her robustly voluptuous frame into flowery designer summer dresses. Occasionally, Lamont remembered, she'd wear a yellow sunflower, or a daisy, even an occasional tulip tucked in her waist-length, voluminous black hair. Her appearance always seemed heavenly, and that had been the reason why he'd loved her so much.

As he parked in front of the house, he hoped with a bit of desperation that she'd be as happy to see him, as he would be her. There was a chance that he might not even be welcome. Standing outside of the car that he'd driven, and staring in awe at the house that had been properly taken care of over the years, he decided that that would just be a chance that he'd have to take.

Lamont rounded the vehicle and made his way up onto the sidewalk.

He stepped up to the three-foot-high gate that guarded the front yard and let himself inside. The grass had been recently cut, but the storm had left it damp and soggy. Using the narrow stone walkway that stretched out before him, he made his way up to the porch. Before he could make his way up the stairs, the door began to slowly open, and in a matter of seconds a petite blond-haired female who appeared to be in her early twenties stood before him.

Her eyes were doe-like and gleamed like green emeralds in her flawless face. She was nearly the same height as he and was taller than any white female that he'd ever encountered before. She had the look of an elegant European, and was apparently an athlete, but when she spoke her accent was American.

"Can I help you?"

Lamont had stopped in his tracks, and was turning to leave, when he stammered,

"I, uh… I think that I might've made a mistake. I don't think that the person that I've come to see lives here anymore."

He turned and began to make a hasty departure.

The girl watched him as he did so, and out of curiosity she took in the appearance of his attire. She paid close attention to his gait and noticed the spring in his step. Then he looked back, and she noticed the way that he twisted his mouth and raised an eyebrow… the same way that her foster brother used to look when he was unsure about something.

"Lamont…" she said in nearly a whisper. Panic kicked in when she realized that he couldn't hear her. "Lamont!" she called out to him, her heart beating wildly inside of her chest.

It was her foster brother… her favorite, and the one she'd loved the most when they had been younger.

Startled, he turned around and glared at her.

"Lamont…it's me, Bridget," she said, her voice betraying her emotions. His eyes grew wide and he stared at her in amazement. "Bridget…Little Bridget? Man, are you serious?"

Lamont's face lit up like the fourth of July, as he made his way back up onto the porch.

Without further hesitation, Bridget threw herself into his open arms. "How've you been?" Lamont asked embracing her warmly. She didn't answer him at first, because she was too busy crying against his chest, causing his heart to ache in return.

"Why are you crying?" he asked her, a bit confused. She couldn't possibly have missed him that much.

"Because…" she said sniffing, "I've always thought that I would never see you again."

"Awe, dang it, Bridget, please stop crying." Pulling herself away from him so that she could look up into his face, she wiped at her eyes to better clear her vision.

"Where have you been?" she asked, sounding a mite angry. "I live over in Jersey, now," he told her, understanding her emotions. He'd left with his brother and had never bothered to contact any of his other siblings, nor Mommy Sylvia for that matter. Even if they had only been his adopted relatives, Bridget had loved him like they'd been around each other for their entire lives. Then, out of nowhere, he'd just up disappeared after school, one day. If she would have never seen him again, she would have never gotten over the loss of him and would have carried that pain with her forever.

"With whom?" she asked. "By yourself?"

"No..." he said with a chuckle. "With Curtis."

"With Curtis. Where is he?" she asked, glancing around as if he might pop up out of nowhere, as Lamont had.

"He's back in Jersey. I drove out here by myself," he told her. Bridget looked past him and saw the Dodge Charger. Without prejudice, she admired the shiny red vehicle that sported black rally stripes, and large chrome custom rims. Then she remembered why Mommy Sylvia had kicked him and his older brother out of the house.

"Whose car is that?" she asked looking back up at him skeptically.

"Oh, that's one of Curtis' cars."

"One of Curtis' cars?"

"Yeah," he told her with nonchalance, unaware of why Curtis having multiple vehicles would be of such a big deal.

"How many does he have?" Bridget asked curiously. Obviously, the drug trade had been very generous to Curtis.

"He owns several, not including the one that I just..."

He paused, and the gesture didn't go unnoticed by Bridget. "Not including the one that you just what?" she asked, her eyebrows rising. "That I wrecked," he told her sullenly. "Oh..." she said surprised, "well, it can't be that big of deal, because he's still allowing you to drive that nice car."

"That's just it, Bridget..." he told her, "he doesn't know." "He doesn't know? Uh oh, Lamont are you okay? I mean, if something's wrong and its led you to stealing your brother's car, after having wrecked one of his other vehicles...if for some reason Curtis has turned on you because of that, then don't worry- I'm here if you need me," she told him.

He sighed, and stared back up at the house, then back down at her.

"Bridget, that's part of the reason why I'm here. Something really bad has happened, and I came because I need to see Mommy Sylvia. I need her advice on something."

Bridget's hand shot to her chest. She stared up into his eyes, as her own misted over. He didn't know.

Lamont gently placed both of his hands on her shoulders, taking note of her sudden change of moods. Whatever had caused the expression on her face was surely something that he needed to brace both himself, and her for.

"Bridget, what's wrong?" he asked, anticipating the news that she was about to deliver. Something was terribly wrong, and the pained expression on her face told him so.

"Lamont...Mommy Sylvia passed over a year ago. She's no longer with us. When she died I took over the house and looked after things for her."

Lamont's mouth fell open in disbelief, and as he stared up at the house that he'd once lived in, and had known genuine kinship and unconditional love in, he regretted not having returned much sooner to visit.

That news had just shattered his spirit, and in defeat he let his head hang low until it rested against Bridget's.

"What am I gonna do, now?" he mumbled.

Bridget slid back into his arms, and they stood like that for nearly ten minutes. She didn't want to let go of Lamont, afraid that he'd disappear into thin air, and she'd never see him again.

One of the neighbors that were out walking their dog strolled by and asked if she were alright. She waved at the middle-age white male and they continued. "Lamont…" she said in a tone so low that it sounded like a whisper, "let's go inside."

Body and spirit totally drained, he allowed her to lead the way.

12

"What are you doing here?" Klick Klak asked angrily.

"Come on…is that how you treat all of your guests?" Officer Sims asked with sarcasm.

"You are not my fucking guest. I don't even know how in the fuck you knew where my family lived. What in the fuck did you do, follow me?"

"More or less…" Officer Sims told him, unaffected by Klick Klak's impoliteness. "You're not a hard person to tail, with all of those luxury vehicles that you have. Nice they are… I could sure use one of those."

"Look…" Klick Klak said through clenched teeth, "I told you that I would take care of you, so you don't have to come around here stalking me and my family."

"Oh, I'm not stalking you. I just wanted to come by and have another little chat with you. I thought that there were some things that you might want to know."

"Like what?" Klick Klak asked, uncertain if he even cared to hear what this piece of shit had to say. Your opposing group of hustlers on the Eastside is planning to make a major attempt to get rid of you," the cop told him. "Tell me something that I don't already know. I ain't worried about that shit. I am the streets… I can take care of mine."

Klick Klak didn't care to discuss the details of the conversation that he'd just had with the fiancée of the leader of his opposing group, so he kept the knowledge of their upcoming alliance to himself. Let the no-teeth bastard think what he wants, Lamont thought. "Well, smart ass, what you don't know is that they've already attacked one of your crew members. Fucked him up pretty badly, too."

"What… what in the fuck are you talking about?"

"Got to your white boy over on North Main. Beat him to a pulp. Left him for dead inside of his apartment. Even had the girl that he sees scared to death, the way they done that boy," he told Klick Klak.

"Who…you mean Jacob? Who done that to Jacob?"

"I Just told you."

"Shit! Shit! Shit! Shit! Shit!" Klick Klak said, placing both of his fists to his forehead and closing his eyes. Jacob was his man, and if Tommy had somehow found a way to get to him then someone was surely going to pay. How in the hell had they gotten to him, anyways? he wondered. He dropped his hands and begun to pace, leaving footprints in the grass that surrounded them. Officer Sims spoke again.

"You want to know what else?"

Until Irene

"Shut the fuck up!" Klick Klak whirled on him.

"Oh, Mr. Crowder, you might want to hear this, as well," he said with a grin.

Klick Klak just stared, his chest rising and falling as if he were out of breath.

Enjoying the moment, Officer Sims told him, "I know who your little brother was scoring his smack from."

"From who?" Klick Klak asked, hating the sight of the corrupt cop now more than ever.

"You should thank Tommy and his boys for that beating that he and his boys delivered to your partner."

"What in the fuck are you trying to say...that it was Jacob supplying my brother?"

Officers Sims' grin returned.

"Get the fuck out of here! I don't believe you!"

Sims shook his head in disappointment.

"You know, boy, you insult me a little too much. This friendship that we have is never going to flourish if you keep that up."

"You stupid...this ain't no fucking friendship," Klick Klak told him angrily. "You are just a fucking dirty cop looking for a payday. I should..."

He began reaching for his gun, but the trained officer was much faster, and had the drop on him in no time.

"Boy, don't you fucking play with me," Sims warned, spittle flying from his mouth in

Page | 101

the process. "I will kill your ass in a fucking heartbeat.

So, you just go on, now, and be stupid."

A deadly silence passed between them, as they stared coldly at one another. A light breeze swept over them, causing Goosebumps to rise on both men's flesh.

Klick Klak's hand fell and rested at his side, and Officer Sims nodded. He holstered his weapon and glared at Curtis with skepticism.

"You know, I didn't think that you'd be this difficult to deal with. You're making this hard on yourself. I've always wondered why you drug dealers do that. Things could be a lot easier for you."

"Oh, yeah… how's that?" Klick Klak asked.

"I thought that I made it clear that if you take care of me, I'll take care of you?'

"If I were to start paying you today, how would I benefit from it?" Klick Klak asked.

"What you don't know is that I've already begun helping your cause, and you haven't paid me shit."

"You have? How?" Klick Klak asked, still not believing anything that this asshole was saying.

The toothless grin returned.

"You'll find out soon enough, boy. Just have my first payment ready for me by the end of this week, or we ain't gon' be so good friends no more."

There was no response from Klick Klak. He was past tired of looking at this man who was an unwanted guest.

"Well…" Officer Sims said, turning his back to Curtis and heading back toward the way that he'd come through the woods, "I guess I'll be getting on ahead now. Don't want to wear out my welcome."

"Too fucking late for that," Klick Klak said, causing Sims to stop in his tracks.

He peered back over his shoulder at Curtis. "Oh and tell you little Italian friend who belongs to ole' Tommy Boy, that I don't think that plan of hers is gonna work. Would be nice, though," he said, as he began walking away, the wind causing his last comment to trail off, and go unheard.

Klick Klak gritted his teeth and wondered how the old bastard had overheard he and Stephanie's conversation when he'd been so far off.

He waited patiently and watched the cop's departure, until the man's baldhead disappeared.

Turning, he looked back up at the house and wasn't surprised when he spotted Denise leaning out of her upstairs bedroom window with a military issued 7.06 MR-50 sniper rifle trained on the section of the wooded area that Officer Sims had made his departure through.

He smiled, and she lowered the weapon. She'd had the drop on the uninvited piece of shit the entire time.

Once again, Curtis was reminded of why he loved this woman.

13

Tommy had just returned from paying his respects to the parents of the young man that had been slain on his block. He'd tried his best to give his condolences, and to assure them that he'd see to it that justice was sought out for their son's death, but they'd not been too receptive to his promises. Both the father and the mother had blamed him for what had happened to their son. They were aware that Tommy was the neighborhood's lead drug dealer and felt that he was entirely at fault. Nothing or no one could have convinced them any differently.

Having taken off alone after the police and paramedics had arrived, he'd made his way to his home on Park Avenue and Madison that he shared with Stephanie. He needed to be in her presence and inside the confines of her home, so that he could do some serious thinking. So much had happened since the arrival of the storm; a storm that at present seemed to have passed. It was nearly impossible to believe that such tragedy had taken place. It took everything inside of Tommy to bury his thoughts of Alaena somewhere deep in the back of his mind. Thinking too much about the death of his sister would only cloud his decision making and push him over the edge. He knew that he couldn't afford that right now; he couldn't go over that cliff. He had to stay focused if he was going to come out of this ordeal victorious. Too much was going on for him to get careless.

Stephanie's guidance was something that he always sought when the game that he played became too much to deal with on his own. Not only was she a great advisor, but she was a good listener as well.

Most of all, what Tommy needed right now, was to vent and he was certain that his woman would be there to lend her ear.

The road passed beneath the wheels of his truck at thirty-five miles per hour. Obscenely vulgar rap music blared through his stereo system and caused a distorted collage of his unwanted thoughts. There was a blur before his eyes, as he maneuvered through traffic on autopilot.

Within the next five minutes, he was pulling up in front of the house.

He immediately took notice of the absence of Stephanie's vehicle. He wondered where she might be, and started to call her cell phone, but changed his mind. He'd just go inside and treat himself to some peace and quiet. Maybe that was really what he needed to relieve some of the tension that he was feeling.

Making his way up the front steps, he unlocked the door and stepped inside. The living room appeared to be just as they'd left it earlier that day; tidy and well-kempt. The central air /heating unit pumped out enough cool air to slow the process of a melting popsicle. The blinds were drawn shut, so that no one could see out, nor anyone in.

Tommy made his way over to their large sectional, and after removing his gun from the small of his back, he flopped down onto it lazily. Lying back, he let the .40 caliber rest on his stomach and closed his eyes. Too restless to sleep, he fought with the barriers inside of his head, before finally giving into the vivid thoughts and images that plagued him.

His mind returned to the urgent phone call that he'd received when he'd been back at Tony's shop. The moment that he'd been told about his sister's death and the shock that he'd felt returned in full force. Images of the actual scene followed, and the pain that he'd been trying to avoid crept its way back into his soul.

He groaned and a jolt of shivers ran through him. Anyone looking in from the outside would have thought that he was cold. Yet, at this very moment, such wasn't the case. The only thing that was beginning to freeze over when it came to Tommy, was his heart. He had tried to fight these emotions off, but the more that he did so, the more that his will seemed to be slipping away. Only more bloodshed would relieve him of his grief, so more bloodshed was what he was going to seek out.

He had thought that, after discussing things over with Stephanie, he'd be able to see a bit of reason out of the current situation. But now that she wasn't here, he was able to think on his own and came to the realization that there was no other way that he and Klick Klak's issues could be handled. They had been mere adversaries before now, but since the late turn of events, they had become more than just enemies. To Tommy, they were more like a demon and an angel; neither would ever be able to coexist with the other. He was certain that one of them had to go. There was no question as to who that one would be, and if there turned out to be anyone else in opposition to him, then they'd get the same amount of what he had in store for Klick Klak and his little brother. There would be no exceptions.

He sat up and reached for the remote to turn the television on but stopped in mid-stride when he heard what sounded like someone moving about inside of his kitchen.

In a flash, he was standing, gun in hand.

He crept toward the kitchen and paused just outside of the entrance, shielding himself behind the wall.

He listened.

The sound of a man coughing and clearing his throat unnerved him. Tommy had no idea who the person inside of his kitchen might be.

He raised his gun high and braced himself, before he swung around into the kitchen. What he saw nearly scared the shit out of him.

There was a baldheaded black cop sitting at his dining table in full dress.

Tommy had no idea who the man was, or his motive for being there, but one thing was for certain… he hadn't been invited.

Nervously, Tommy kept his gun hand rigid, and trained his sights on the cop.

Officer Sims smiled.

Tommy grimaced.

"What in the fuck are you doing in my house, pig?"

"You ever seen a toothless pig devour its meal?"

"What?"

"Have you ever seen a toothless pig devour its meal?" Sims asked again.

"No, man, what in the fuck are you talking about?'

"Well, boy, if you don't point that damn gun away from me, then you're going to learn that there's a first time for everything."

Tommy flinched, then waited. Ten seconds passed, before he complied.

"Now, have a seat," Officer Sims motioned to one of Tommy's dining chairs.

"I'll stand."

Officer Sims watched him carefully, making several mental notes. Already, he didn't like the kid and he immediately came to the assumption that Tommy was going to be a problem.

"Suit yourself...it's your house, but since I can see that we're not going to be friends, allow me to cut to the chase. You, buddy-boy, need to leave well-enough alone, and let us deal with the situation involving your sister's death."

"What?" Tommy asked angrily. He glared at the toothless cop skeptically, and in a matter of seconds, it hit him. "Wait a minute...I remember you. You're the cop that was at the scene of the accident."

Officer Sims nodded.

"Well, why are you here? To tell me that shit? Y'all motherfuckers didn't do your job, but now you want to tell me what to fucking..."

"That's right, boy, I'm telling you!" Officer Sims spat, as he stood.

"I'm telling you to back the fuck off of the Crowder Boys...leave that to us."

"How do you know that I haven't already? Fuck you doing...following me?"

Officer Sims dug into his pockets and Tommy watched him carefully. He removed a Polaroid photo and tossed it on the table. Gun still at his side, Tommy strolled over and picked it up. His facial expression turned into a scowl, and he glared back up at the cop.

"Who the fuck is this?"

"Don't play with me...you know exactly who the fuck that is."

It was a photo of Tommy's cousin, Jacob, and it showed the aftereffects of the beating that he'd taken.

"Pretty nice work that you and your boys did, if I do say so myself."

Tommy flicked the picture back at him.

"You can't prove shit."

That toothless grin returned.

"Don't need to, and ain't trying to. Just letting you know that I'm on your ass."

His smile faded. "Just stay away from those other boys."

"And if I don't…what?" Tommy asked challenging him.

The black man's hand returned back into his pocket. Once again, Tommy watched him carefully as another picture was taken out and tossed onto his dining table. He picked it up and instinctively his gun hand began to twitch, but Sims was a fraction of a second too fast for him. A 357 Ruger was now pointed dead center at Tommy's head. His hand slackened and the .40caliber pistol that he held fell noisily to the floor.

"The Italian fellas told me to tell you and your crew that you have got twenty-four hours to get off of that block…or else…"

"Or else what?" Tommy asked glaring at him hatefully.

"You're not blind, although, the next one will be much worse,"

Officer Sims warned.

"He was just a kid," Tommy said angrily.

"On the wrong team-at the wrong time."

"You killed him with a fucking baseball bat."

Next time will be worse."

There was a deadly silence that passed between them.

"Twenty-four hours…" Sims told him again. "They pay me well, and I take my money seriously."

Tommy said nothing. He only glared at the cop that he now knew he'd kill before it was all said and done.

He watched through bloodshot vision, as Officer Sims moved carefully around him. His gun still aimed as he headed for the front exit.

Sims disappeared into the living room, and seconds passed before the front door clicked shut. Vexed beyond reason, Tommy knelt to pick up his gun, and for the first time that day, he thought of murdering someone else other than Curtis and Lamont Crowder.

14

Back in Queens, Lamont and Bridget were sitting at the dining room table that they'd once sat down at for a many of dinners together when they were young. It had been years since they'd last sat at that table together. The last time that they'd shared a family dinner Mommy Sylvia had been there and had prepared them a large enough meal to feed all of her adopted children and any number of guests that they might have had. It didn't feel right sitting there, without her, and Lamont told Bridget of his discomfort.

"It's awkward being here, and not being able to see Mommy Sylvia. I don't think that I can even remember a time in this house when she wasn't here with us except for when she was at work."

Sitting next to Lamont she reached over and took his hand from where it lay on top of the table and intertwined their fingers. She laid her head comfortably on his shoulder.

"I know…" she told him, "I have to deal with my emotions because of her absence every day. There are some mornings that I wake up, and it's like I can still smell her perfume."

"Damn, Bridget…I'm sorry," Lamont told her.

"It's okay…I guess. I just miss her is all. Since everyone else got grown and moved out to start their adult lives, it's been kind of lonely around here, you know. Other than work, I'm here nearly all of the time tending to the house."

"You mean to tell me that you're here by yourself all of the time?" he asked.

Bridget nodded.

"You've done a good job keeping the house up," he told her.

"Thank you."

"I'm sorry that I didn't think to come sooner. I've just been so busy and caught up in school that I…I don't know… forgot."

"By the way, how are you doing in school?" she asked sitting up straight, so that she could look into his eyes.

"Well, I've been doing great. I've got good grades. I'm playing sports, and I've actually been offered several football scholarships that I've been mulling over," he said the last part with a bit of hesitation, and Bridget didn't miss it.

"But?" she asked.

Sighing, Lamont dropped his head, and Bridget squeezed his hand for assurance.

"But I messed up," he said looking back up at her. "I messed up really bad, Bridget."

The way that he'd said the word 'bad' disturbed her, so she looked away for a second to gather her wits, before she asked,

"What do you mean? How bad, Lamont?"

Studying her face, he wondered if he should trouble her with his problems. It had been so long since he'd last seen Bridget, and he loved her deeply. She had always been the homebody amongst them all when they were younger, and knowing that she had never been one to venture out into the streets, he was reluctant to even relay any details about the kind of life that he'd begun to live to her. Although, that was why he had come to speak to Mommy Sylvia. Only, she wasn't there anymore. She wasn't going to walk through the door and embrace him the way he'd hoped for. She was never coming back to be a foster mother to him, as she had once been.

But Bridget on the other hand, was exactly where he needed her, and she was showing him the same amount of concern as Mommy Sylvia would have. Confused and exhausted, Lamont relented. "I started selling heroin, Bridget."

Her hand clenched around his, and she stared at him evenly, while trying to conceal her shock. She hadn't been expecting what he'd just told her.

Turning so that her entire body was facing him, she asked,

"There's a lot more to this story isn't there, Lamont?"

Squeezing his eyes shut, he nodded.

Bridget said nothing more, as she waited for him to continue.

"I had an accident this morning while I was out taking care of some business, and…someone died," he told her.

She gasped, and for a fraction of a second, her hand slackened inside of his.

"Oh, my God…Lamont, how did it happen?"

"I was driving Curtis' Benz, and I dropped my phone in the floorboard in an attempt to answer an incoming call. Reaching down to pick it up, I somehow lost control of the car. It all happened so fast that I didn't have enough time to think about what I was doing. All I remember is that I swerved and collided into something hard. After the collision, I don't know how long I had been unconscious, but when I woke up, I was both stunned, and disoriented. I managed to climb out of the car, and when I did, I found… I found…" Lamont tried to tell her, but he couldn't finish.

"You found what?" Bridget asked, although, she immediately wished that she hadn't.

"A little girl lying dead up under the car."

Bridget sucked in a sharp breath of air, and this time she did release his hand, though, only to steady herself from the sudden surge of shock that she felt.

"Oh, my goodness, Lamont, that's horrible!"

"Bridget, you don't understand the depths of what I've done. By doing what I did, I've started a war between Curtis and his hustling rival; a war that will only end up in more bloodshed. It's all my fault."

Bridget saw the sudden look of fright in his eyes, and it scared her. Without thinking, she leaned forward and embraced him. She pressed her cheek to his and hugged him tightly.

Lamont clung to her like his life depended on it, and all of his emotions came crashing down on him. The smell of Bridget's Christian Dior perfume and the scent of her lilac shampoo invaded his senses. The contours of her body pressed firmly against him, creating a distraction that made him nearly forget why he had come. She shifted and her face raised a fraction. With her lips pressed lightly against his ear, she told him, "Oh, Lamont, you don't have to be afraid…I'm here for you, and I always will be."

Lamont hadn't realized when he'd gone from slightly shaking, to panting. His body was beginning to react in ways that he hadn't expected it to. Without thinking, his hands moved freely across her upper and lower back, and Bridget's response to his touch was disarmingly receptive.

"I've missed you so much…you don't have any idea," she confessed, as her right hand crept upward to rest on the back of his neck.

Moving ever so slightly, his breath caught when her lips touched his cheek in a whisper of a kiss. He could feel her breathing heavily against him. Without thinking, he turned his face toward her, and that did it. Their lips touched and explosives went off between them. The room spun and Bridget climbed all of the way into Lamont's lap to better support herself.

There was no turning back, as recollection of their actions overtook them both. Neither of them was willing to break a kiss that they both knew that they shouldn't be sharing. They had once been foster brother and sister. Though, Bridget had always secretly loved Lamont in a much more intimate way.

Back when they were growing up, she'd been too young-minded and shy to reveal her true feelings toward someone that she knew she shouldn't desire in such an un-lady-like manner. But, now that they were both adults, and were no longer bonded as they had been before, Bridget no longer felt the need to restrain herself. She wouldn't pass up the only man that she'd ever loved.

Their kissing took on a feverish pitch, and their pace quickened. Lamont's arms wrapped tightly around Bridget, as he held her close. He could feel the swell of her breast pressed up against him.

His breathing turned heavy, and at that very moment he moaned in pleasure. He wondered what had gotten into him. For years he'd harbored his intimate feelings for the gorgeous European girl-keeping them a secret and hidden within himself. He'd always felt it was wrong to feel the way that he had about someone that was raised by the same parent as he, no matter the differences between the blood that ran through their veins. As an adolescent, he'd had a ridiculously large crush on Bridget, but when he and Curtis had moved out on their own, and so much time had passed between them, he'd honestly began to put his silly feelings behind him, chalking them up as a mere childhood infatuation. But now that he was here with Bridget and she was wrapped in his arms and straddling his waist like an excited cowgirl-his desire for her was vastly returning, and all of his thoughts of decency were going out of the window.

Lamont hoped that he wasn't making a mistake by acting on his feelings, because Bridget had once been someone very special to him. She squirmed and he mistook her impatience for less restrained compassion as a request to be set free.

With a start, he broke the kiss and turned her loose. Leaning away from her, he thought that he saw disgust on her face.

"I'm...I'm sorry, Bridget. I didn't mean to do that," he blurted.

She stared back at him stunned. "What... you're sorry? Why'd you stop?" she asked, grabbing ahold of his shirt, and trying to pull him back toward her.

Lamont didn't budge. He was confused.

"What…you're not mad at me?"

Bridget's frown turned into a grin.

"Lamont…do you know how long I've waited for that kiss?"

"Huh?" he asked.

"Oh, my God, did you not ever realize when we were younger that I've always liked…no, loved you?" she asked him.

"Wait a minute…are you serious?" he asked not believing that he'd heard her correctly. "Never before have I been so serious in my life."

"Awe, man, this is crazy," he said, finally having something to feel good about since the accident. He couldn't believe in his good fortune, having been reunited with Bridget. Even though he'd come to find out the unfortunate news about the passing of Mommy Sylvia, he'd been blessed with the unexpected presence of the most important person that had been missing in his life. Without her, he'd been incomplete. She had been the missing piece to his entire being when they'd been younger. Even back when they had attended school together, she'd always been the one to help him maintain his grades. Bridget didn't know it, but because of her he was now presented with the privilege of attending just about any division 1 college that he so chose to in both the state of New Jersey, and New York. Yet, up until this point, none of that had really mattered to him. He'd not even been sure about pursuing his promised collegiate career as a football player.

Being here with Bridget, though, all of the irresponsible things that he'd done began to plague him, and Lamont wondered how disappointed she might be in him if she knew the rest of his troubling story.

Lamont wasn't yet sure if he should make his entire confession to her, but there was one thing that he knew for certain; he wasn't going to pass up on having something special with Bridget any longer.

"Bridget, I have always felt the same exact way about you. I was just afraid to make it known back then."

"Oh, Lamont..." she said, her heart leaping for joy. She leaned in and kissed him gently on the lips. When she broke the kiss, they stared deeply into one another's eyes.

Without any further words spoken, Bridget stood and took Lamont by the hand. Allowing her to lead, he stood as well.

For the both of them, time stood still. There was an air of understanding between man and woman at that very moment that could have only been shared between the two of them. Somehow, destiny and fate had found its way into their lives and had made them whole where they had once been so incomplete. Here was where they both knew that they were meant to be. And there were no longer any barriers to keep them from one another. The time was now, and both Bridget and Lamont were sure of it.

With a soulful attachment that was about to become as solid as a lock and key, Fate led her Destiny toward the rear of the house, where her bedroom awaited them for as long as need be.

15

Curtis drove down North Main and parked in front of his twenty-four-hour corner store that he and one of his business cronies owned together. He had fifty percent ownership of the establishment, which was a well-received convenience for the local citizens. The person that he'd gone into business with was a young black man the same age as him by the name of James Perry.

Curtis had known James for just about all of his life. They'd gone to the same schools together, had nearly all of the same classes, and had played on the same basketball teams throughout both middle school and high school. From doubling up on dates with girls, to going in half on quarter-brick of cocaine, they'd done it all as two-man team. Since they were older and had built a mini army of die-hard hustlers, they were enjoying the fruits of their labors without remorse. At least, that was the case until the late turn of events that were putting all that Curtis had managed to build through blood sweat, and tears in jeopardy.

It was time for his weekly check-in with James. He needed to find out what kind of profits they'd brought in for the week. Plus, he wanted to ask what kind of profits they'd brought in for the week. Plus, he wanted to ask around and see if news of Tommy's little sister's accidental death had made it to the hood yet. If it hadn't, then he knew that it would eventually. It was safe for him to say that there was an ensuing war headed straight for them and their territory, in the near future. Not only had they managed to nearly obliterate all of Tommy's Eastside heroin clientele, but they'd also caused the rival kingpin a great amount of grief by robbing him of a very close relative. Or at least Curtis' little brother had.

He entered the store and glanced observantly. There were several customers roaming the well-stocked aisles, undoubtedly on emergency runs while the storm was in its state of dormancy.

Looking toward the checkout counter, he spotted the Laotian clerk that James had hired six months back. Teresa was currently a psychology major at Passaic County Community College, and also a very hard and reliable worker. Curtis really liked her and had he not been so in love with Denise, then he probably would have asked her out on a date; a date that he knew she wouldn't refuse.

Approaching Teresa, he masked his current distress by putting on his best smile and dredging up what little bit kindly spirits that he had left in him.

"Teresa how are you, today?" he asked.

She smiled at him from behind the counter.

"I'm doing fine, Curtis. How are you?"

"I'm managing."

He took notice of her new hairstyle, which she now wore cut closely. It was a style that he'd never seen her sport before, and it suited her well. She sorts of resembled an Asian Halle Berry. The hairdo made her face look both femininely strong and beautiful at the same time. The eyeglasses that she wore gave her a distinct look of intelligence. Hot and sexy were the two words that would have best described her at present.

"I like your hair," he told her, and watched in amusement as the expression on her face turned into an attractive ball of sunshine.

"Thank you," she told him, unable to conceal her appreciation for his compliment. She wondered if he knew how much she secretly desired his companionship.

"How are things going around here this week?" he asked.

"Well, other than all of the rain that we've been getting, which has been causing the delivery trucks to arrive late, things have been pretty good.

I really can't wait until this storm passes over," she told him.

"Yeah, as quiet as it's been for the past couple of hours, you would think that we've seen the worst of it, but the weatherman says otherwise.

"There hasn't been any trouble around here lately, has there?" Teresa chuckled.

"Yeah, right...not with those guys that you have out there on the corner. I don't think anybody's stupid enough to come around here starting trouble. Those are some crazy friends that you have out there."

Curtis maintained his smile.

"Loyal, yeah...crazy, nah. They're just down for their 'hood, and what we all stand for. They don't be bothering you, do they?'

"No. No. No..." she told him reassuring, "they rarely even come in here, unless it's to get something to drink, or some cigars."

He nodded.

"What about any unfamiliar faces? Anyone come through here that you've not seen before... anyone that looked out of place?"

"No," she said shaking her head.

"No police, either?"

Teresa's smile faded.

"No... none that I can remember."

There was a look of concern on her face, now.

"Curtis, is something wrong? Is everything alright?"

Unconsciously, he'd allowed his smile to slip away, and he immediately regretted it.

"Oh, yeah...yeah, Teresa, everything's good," he lied. "I'm just wondering, you know..."

She opted not to pry any further, although, she watched him carefully. It was apparent that something was amiss, and Curtis didn't feel comfortable discussing it with her. The fact that he might not trust her was a total disappointment. She wondered if she'd ever done anything to make him feel that way.

A verting his gaze from Teresa's beautiful piercing eyes, he looked toward the back of the store where James' office was located.

"Where's 'J.P'... he here?" he asked her.

"Huh unh... he stepped out earlier... said that her was heading home to check on his girl and kid," she told him.

"Damn...I really needed to holler at him, too," he stressed.

Teresa's eyes narrowed and she stepped a little closer to Curtis. She placed a gentle hand on his forearm, and told him, "Curtis, if there's something wrong and I can be of any help, you can talk to me. I'm sure that you know by now that you can trust me."

He looked down at her delicate hand on his arm, and just as he was about to give in, the door swung open and one of his goons came rushing inside.

It was a Puerto Rican kid named Hi-low, and it took several seconds before he could speak, as he fought to catch his breath. When he finally managed to do so, there was urgency in his voice.

"Aye yo, Klick Klak, they...they got Jay Hood! They got Jay Hood, son... hemmed him up on the block with ten bundles, but I think that they are fucking robbing him, or something! They are robbing him, son!"

"They're robbing him. Who in the fuck are they?"

"The jakes, son!"

"What...the jakes? Shit, how many of them is it?" Curtis asked concerned. Jay Hood was the second in command since the hospitalization of Jacob. He was one of the men that he distributed most of his dope to on consignment.

"Yo, it's only one, yo. Some big black, bald, no teeth motherfucka!"

"No teeth...man, fuck! I'm getting tired of this motherfucka!"

"You know who it is?" Teresa asked him with alarm in her voice, but Curtis ignored her inquiry, and headed for the door.

Stepping outside, he made a right turn and looked annoyingly up the block. About a hundred yards out, he could see Officer Sims climbing back into his cruiser.

"Hey!" Curtis yelled angrily, but Sims began to pull off. He stood watching heatedly as the dirty cop drove off and nearly exploded with rage at the sight of Sims' middle finger sticking disrespectfully out of the driver side window.

16

Tommy was sitting nervously inside of the kitchen, when he heard the front door shut. He jumped to his feet and headed for the living room. His anxiety subsided once he saw that it was only Stephanie, although, he was still agitated by the unexpected visitor that he'd had earlier, and it was evident in his tone when he spoke to her.

"Where have you been?"

Stephanie was headed towards him when he inquired about her whereabouts but stopped in mid-stride to assess his demeanor. He appeared upset, and she wondered if he'd already known where she'd been.

"I went to see… a friend," she told him.

"Damn, girl, you could have at least called and told me that you weren't going to be here when I got home. I've been waiting around for you for hours."

His angered words reminded her all that he'd been through, and she immediately regretted having left his side for part of the day. Although, she wasn't quite that certain that she'd had any other choice but to. She'd made that trip out to see Klick Klak's baby's mom for him.

"Awe, honey, I'm sorry," she said closing the distance between the two of them and wrapping her arms around his waist. "I shouldn't have left your side. I truly apologize," she said looking up into his eyes.

Tommy returned her embrace and gazing down at his fiancee and taking notice of her

angelic features, his nerves calmed, and he thought better of his complaints toward her. He wondered what would have happened had she been the one to come home first and found the black cop sitting inside of their kitchen as if he were at home   . It frightened him to think that the toothless animal might have harmed his precious lady. He made the decision then there to keep the uninvited government official's presence inside of their home to himself, not wanting to trouble her with the disturbing news.

He leaned forward and she rose up on her tiptoes so that they could share a kiss. Several minutes passed before he released her.

"Come into the kitchen, honey, and let me make you something to eat," she told him soothingly.

Tommy followed her without protest.

He found his seat that he'd occupied before she'd returned home and watched as Stephanie laid her Chanel shoulder bag on top of the counter, then made her way over to the refrigerator. She paused as she peered inside, and he was once again caught up in her beauty. There was an illuminating ray of sunshine coming in through an overhead window that had been designed to brighten up the room and its facilities, as was the very case at present, and it bathed her creamy features in a sea of golden dust. Her hair was a silky black and hung loosely down her back, curling without prejudice wherever it so chose to. She was truly breathtaking, and Tommy had no clue as to what he'd do, or what he'd become if he were to ever lose her.

"So, where have you been?" he asked quietly, and it was apparent to Stephanie that there was no accusation in his tone.

She found what she'd been in search of and placed it on the counter beside the island. Reaching inside several of the cabinets before her, she removed several dry goods and appliances that she would need to prepare their meal.

Busying herself, Stephanie kept her back to Tommy, as she made her best attempt to provide him with an answer to his inquiry.

"Tommy…do you trust me?"

"Yes, Steph… you know I do."

He wondered why she'd responded to his question with one of her own.

"You sure? Do you really trust me?"

"Yeah, Babe…" he told her, watching her intently as she moved gracefully and deliberately through the golden haze. It was amazing how the storm that had once haunted them had abruptly subsided.

"Do you trust my judgement?" she asked, and that set Tommy on alert. Stephanie's tone had taken on a hint of nervousness, and Tommy hadn't missed it.

He stood and made his way across the room, stopping when he was standing directly behind her. She paused when she felt his hands on her waist but continued when he bent and kissed the nape of her neck.

"Why are you asking me these questions?" he asked her softly; his lips near her ear. "You know that I trust you, Steph."

The margarine that she'd placed in the skillet began to sizzle and its garlic scent filled the room with a delicious aroma. She sprinkled a pinch of parsley and cilantro into the pan, and then began to lay several raw boneless chicken strips inside the buttered seasoning. While the meat cooked slowly, she began to prep several side dishes for their meal.

She was trying to prolong the answer to his last question for as long as possible, because she was afraid of what his reaction might be to what she knew she had to tell him.

Tommy was growing impatient.

"Stephanie…"

"Tommy, I went to see someone, today."

"Someone like who, babe?"

"Klick Klak's baby mother," she confessed in a clipped tone.

Stephanie regretted the words as soon as they slipped from her lips.

He whirled her around to face him, and with a snap he spoke harshly to his angel.

"What? What the fuck do you mean? I know that you didn't just say what the fuck I think that you did?"

"Tommy, hon, I only did it because..."

"Because what?" he asked cutting her off. "What in the fuck were you thinking by going over there? That's the ole' lady of my fuckin' enemy, and you just waltzed your little ass over there without me knowing. Are you fucking stupid, or something?"

"Tommy, no... and you don't have to talk to me like that! I was only trying to diffuse the oncoming trouble between you and..."

"No one told you to do anything, Stephanie! You don't take it upon yourself to make decisions like that because that shit could've backfired. We are at war! What if those motherfuckers would have thought to kidnap you, or worse? You could have really jeopardized what me and my crew have worked hard to build. Don't you see how stupid that was?"

Stephanie took deep breaths as she fought to keep control of her emotions. She refused to cry under the current circumstances.

"I was only trying to help."

"Oh, yeah, you fucking helped alright. You just made me look like a vulnerable sitting duck is what you did. They just killed my sister!" he screamed at her.

"It was an accident!" she pleaded, hoping desperately that he'd understand her motives more clearly.

"No..." he said venomously, "it ain't going down like that. Those motherfuckers are gonna pay for what they did."

"Please...Tommy..." Stephanie said, reaching up to caress his face. She knew then that she shouldn't say anymore, because there was no use. She'd keep the discussion that she and Curtis had had to herself and would only hope for the best to come out of their situation.

Shoving her hands away, Tommy glared at his fiancée hatefully, before turning on his heels and storming off.

When the front door slammed shut Stephanie broke out in tears.

It was quiet inside of the hospital room. Ieshia's nerves were a wreck.

She had been sitting beside Jacob's bed in the intensive care unit for several hours now, and he'd yet to awaken. The doctors had said that it could take from a day to a year before he came out of his coma. They'd informed her of the fact that he'd suffered trauma to just about his entire body, and that he was indeed lucky that there wasn't any internal bleeding.

She was growing weary sitting there watching his emotionless battered face and the beeping monitor that revealed an unsteady heart rate. She'd given up on calling the man back that she'd spoken to after she'd gone through Jacob's phone and had redialed the last known caller's digits for the time being, because he was no longer answering her calls. She was beginning to suspect that whoever the gentleman was more than likely had something to do with the reason why Jacob was in the position that he was in, or knew something more about it. She wasn't sure about what role he played in the matter, but she was certain that he knew something, and that's why he was avoiding her.

Ieishia knew that she could have given the police a statement when they'd come to question her, but that went against all that she'd been taught growing up. There were ways to get matters like this taken care of, and snitching wasn't one of them.

It didn't help that the person who had done this to her lover was his blood cousin. She didn't want to believe that Tommy could be as vicious as he had, but there was no denying what her eyes had beheld. Her hatred for the person that she'd once considered family was now imminent. She'd never feel the same about Tommy again. If she could avenge Jacob herself, she would. She'd kill Tommy for what he and his heartless entourage of thugs had done. But the fact that she was a pessimist deterred her from even believing that she could be successful in doing harm to someone as malicious as he.

Her only other option, at present, was to pray. So, in pure desperation and total submission, Ieisha dropped down onto her knees at the foot of Jacob's bed, and began to do so. She was two minutes into her petition to God when the electrocardiograph machine began to beep erratically.

Back inside of his corner store, Klick Klak sat inside of his and James' office going through some financial records. Tax time was nearing, and it was his duty to see to it that Uncle Sam got his share of their profits.

Even though he sat in a small room filled with silence, Klick Klak's concentration had long been compromised by the recollection of the humorless use of excessive force by Officer Sims. His patience for the corrupt, money hungry government official was running thin. He didn't know how much more he could take from the toothless piece of shit. His plate was already full and beginning to run over, with all of the problems that he was now undergoing with Lamont.

Klick Klak ran a hand over his recently groomed hair and sighed. Growing irritated, he slammed down the file that he'd been going through and looked up when the door opened with a click, and J.P. walked inside.

Relieved that his friend was finally joining him, he slumped back in his chair.

"Yo, what's up, Klak? How long have you been here?" James asked.

He reached across the desk and pounded fists with his business partner.

"About an hour," Curtis told him. "Yo, I've been trying to figure out these numbers, so that we can take care of this tax shit, but man, my mind is in a fucking maze of shambles right now."

James nodded with understanding and crossing his arms he told Curtis what he'd heard about the late turn of events.

"My dude, I heard about the crazy shit that happened to that little girl and I think that this shit is kind of fucked up even if she was that clown, Tommy's sister."

Curtis looked away for a split second, then back at J.P.

"Yo, you know that cat wants war, right?" he asked.

James frowned.

"Yeah, I already know that much, especially after what that motherfucker and his boys did to his own cousin."

"Are you talking about Jake?" Curtis asked.

"Yeah, man...they say that Jake is lying up in the hospital, right now, in a fucking comatose."

"Motherfucka!" Klick Klak growled, slamming his fist down forcefully onto the desk. "Yo, son, them cats wanna bring it like that, then I'ma give it to them! They don't know who they're fucking with, son...that's my word!"

"Yo, Klak, I feel you, kid. Can you believe that those dudes had the audacity to come over here on our turf and do that shit? They seem to be getting mad brave, son," J.P. goaded, hoping that Curtis was ready as he to retaliate for what had been done. He'd been infuriated and had felt totally disrespected by the 'D-Pound Crew' when he'd first learned of what they'd done to Jacob.

"And to think…" Klick Klak said with a scowl. "I was gonna consider cutting them pussies some slack."

"Cutting them some slack…how? What do you mean?" J.P. asked confused.

Klick Klak looked up at him sternly and confessed.

"Yo, the dude Tommy's girl came by Denise's crib and said that she needed to talk to me. She asked me to hear her out, so I did. She said that she had a solution to our differences. Said that she believed that if I were to raise my heroin prices to match those of the 'D-Pound Crew's', then Tommy and his people would be able to eat again, and there would be no more reason for us to beef."

James was shaking his head already.

"She said that, once me and her dude was on even grounds, then she was certain he and I could run the city together. Yo, the broad was adamant that her plan would work."

"And you were considering this shit?" J.P. asked in disbelief.

Klick Klak broke his gaze from his partner and stared back down at the paperwork in front of him.

J.P. uncrossed, then crossed his arms again. He was silently venting over what Klick Klak had just told him. He couldn't believe that his boy would have even considered such a thing. He would've hated to think that Klick Klak was going soft because of someone's untimely death. Shit happened in the 'hood... that's just the way that life was, sometimes. The good always died young.

"Man, I hope not, Klak, because some shit just ain't meant to be. Like clicking up with those Eastside motherfuckas. We're the Westside, kid. We don't need no collabos. We gone eat over here regardless."

Curtis looked up with an irritated expression.

"Aye yo, you don't have to tell me that shit. I know who we are and what the fuck we're capable of. Did you forget that I started this 'One-Two Live' shit?"

J.P. realized that he'd offended his friend, and immediately retracted his words.

"My bad, son...I ain't mean to offend you, bruh. It's just that 'One-Two Live' is what I stand for. These westside streets is all I know... and I wouldn't be able to deal with it if I had to share our reign with any of those off-brand suckers."

Curtis' tensed expression subsided a bit, though, his brow remained furrowed.

"Yeah, I know what you mean, and you're right. We wouldn't be able to coexist with them motherfuckers. They're not built like us. Shit, it ain't my fault that those clowns ain't eatin. My 'hood is good over here, ya heard."

"That's what the fuck I'm talkin' about," J.P. said, relieved that he'd been able to coax his boy to realization. He'd been afraid that Tommy's little sister's death might have compromised their general's thoroughness. There was no way in hell that he'd let Klick Klak go out like that.

"So, what do you think I should do, J.P.? You think that I should go and get at their click right now, or should I wait until shit cools off before I make a move," Curtis asked, looking at James seriously.

A devilish glare appeared in James' eyes, and he grinned mischievously.

"Yo, I think that you should hit that clown where it hurts most, and as soon as possible."

They stared at one another for several seconds, before Klick Klak nodded.

"Yeah... that's what I'ma do, then... hittem where it hurts...asap."

He dropped his gaze back to the paperwork that sat in front of him, and before he began working on their taxes again, he added, "And I know just where to start."

17

Lamont and Bridget were enjoying one another's company, as they sat cuddled on the living room sofa. Like two long lost lovers, they'd spent the past several hours in one another's arms. Now, they were pretty adamant on not letting each other go. They'd shared something very special in their lovemaking; forming a bond by sharing a sense of familiarity that could have never been achieved, had they both been with someone else.

Lamont had provided Bridget with the fulfillment that she'd always desired in his absence, and she had been able to give him the sense of love, peace, and emotional security that he lacked at present.

Lamont knew that if he were to leave there without her, now, then he'd probably not make it back to Paterson to face his qualms. He had no clue as to how Curtis would react once he found out about Jacob and that his close friend had been the person supplying his little brother with his drugs. He was sure that Curtis would be pissed. With Bridget there, Lamont knew that he'd be able to deal with his brother's anger.

He looked down to where Bridget lay with her head resting on his chest. She was wearing a snug white tee shirt, and a pair of gray cutoffs sweat shorts. She looked relaxed and sexy; her blond mane tied back into a long French braid.

Lamont kissed her forehead, and she stirred.

Gazing up into his eyes, she smiled.

"I've really missed you, Lamont," she told him.

"Bridget, I'm not gonna lie… I've only realized, now, how much I've missed you. I'm sort of mad that we had to get split up, but in a way I'm glad, also, because if we hadn't of…" he smiled and kissed her lips, "then we'd still be brother and sister."

"Yeah…" she said giggling, "that would have really sucked."

He laughed.

"Lamont…"

"Hmm?"

"You know that I love you, right?" she asked him.

There was silence before he spoke.

"Yeah, Bridge, I know…you always have, and I love you, too."

"Not like a sister anymore, though, right?" she asked.

"Hell no…" he told her with a chuckle, and she laughed as well.

He caressed her cheek, as she stared up into his eyes with intensity.

"After what we've just shared, there's no way that I can ever look at you like that again. I think that it's safe enough to say that we're on a whole 'nother level, now."

"You serious?" she asked hoping that he was and craned her neck so that she could look into his eyes.

"Yeah…" he told her, "I don't mean that you have to come and stay, or anything, but would you like to go back with me for a couple of days?"

"Lamont…yes," she said raising herself up into a sitting position and peering down at him. She placed a hand on his bare chest. "I would love to go with you back to your home."

He reached up and touched the side of her face.

"You're serious, aren't you?"

"What…are you kidding me? Of course, I'm serious," she told him.

"I'm not letting you out of my sight."

Lamont rose so that their faces were only inches apart.

"Well, then, I guess we should be getting on up and heading that way.

I know that Curtis probably thinks that I've run away, and ain't coming back."

Bridget shook her head, sympathizing with his unfortunate current disposition.

"I'm not gonna lie, though, I have thought about it."

"No..." she said in disbelief. With gentleness that sent butterflies all throughout his being, she leaned in and kissed his lips. "Lamont, it can't really be that bad."

Staring into her eyes, he gave her a look that said differently.

"Well..." she said, "I'm going back with you. I'm sure that whatever you're going through, we'll be able to get through it together." Placing his forehead against her, he said, "I hope you're right... because if not, then we're in for one helluva storm."

Back on Elmwood Drive, the sun continued to peek out over the picturesque townhomes, giving the neighborhood a serene feel to it. There were a few clouds that drifted overhead in a jumble, yet they were white as snow, and didn't seem threatening in any way.

Inside Denise's home she busied herself with the dinner that she was preparing for herself, her daughter, and Curtis.

Currently, Shakira was upstairs taking a nap in her room, as well as was their dog, Tyson. It had been an hour since she'd taken them up, and she was enjoying the quietness that was rarely a given when the two energetic balls of fire were up and about.

The house smelled delicious, and its aroma slipped through the kitchen's cracked windows and seeped outdoors.

All throughout Elmwood Drive, Denise was known for her soulful cooking. She was constantly praised for her ability to fill someone's stomach with her deliciously delicate entrees. It was believed that none of the women on this side of town could match her skills. Whenever there was some kind of local event being held within their neighborhood, she was always asked to oversee the food that would be prepared and provided for hundreds of people. Even white people loved her cooking, which was a rarity for her, because she'd never known how they'd prepared their food inside of their own homes, until she'd moved out to Elmwood.

The gift that had been passed down to her by her grandmother had made her one of the neighborhood's favorites. There wasn't a man, woman, or child in Elmwood that didn't like Denise.

They knew her as a sweet, lovingly considerate woman and mother. No one knew about her surreptitious life that she shared with her child's father, but even if they had she'd probably still be accepted without question. She was just that important to their community and was in fact highly aware of it. That's why when someone rang her doorbell and she went to answer it, she was confused when she found that no one was there.

Shaking her head, she returned back to her kitchen. Making her way over to the stove, she was just about to open up the oven and check on her string bean casserole when the doorbell rang again.

"Damn it…" she said tossing her oven mitts onto the countertop.

Back inside of the living room, she gazed through the peephole, and immediately became both aggravated and alarmed.

Once again, there was no one there.

Stepping to the side, she peeled the curtains back and looked out over the yard.

Nothing.

"What the hell…" she said out loud.

In frustration, her fists balled at her sides, as she headed for the kitchen. On cue the buzzer on the oven's timer sounded off, and Tyson could be heard scratching on Shakira's bedroom door, upstairs.

"Uh…" she said irritated, "I hate it when that dog does that."

Shutting off the timer, she opened up the oven and peered inside. Satisfied with what she saw, Denise smiled. She reached for the oven mitts, just as Tyson began barking loudly.

A large, strong hand covered hers and startled, she jumped back.

Frightened, she stared into the eyes of an intruder.

"Hello there, Mrs. Crowder…smells downright delicious in here.

What are we havin'?"

"What are you doing in my home?" she asked with exasperation. He ignored her question, and stepping away from her, he inspected the covered dishes that had been set out neatly on top of the dining table.

Out of instinct, she glanced at the kitchen's storage closet where she kept her handgun and was just about to make a dash toward it, but the intruder was surprisingly aware of her thoughts.

In several long strides, he was once again standing in front of her. "Don't do anything stupid, Mrs. Crowder."

Under the kitchen's lighting his baldhead shined like a waxed Milk Dud.

Denise shivered, and he grinned devilishly at her, revealing his toothless smile.

"What the fuck are you doing in my house?" she asked demandingly. With lightning speed, one of his roughly calloused hands reached out and encircled her throat. Lightly, he squeezed, but to Denise it felt like her neck was going to snap off.

"You and your damn boyfriend are some of the rudest people that I know, you know that? You should learn to be more polite and respectful toward your guests," he told her mockingly, and his grip tightened. Denise gagged for air in desperation, and a tear slid down her cheek as she fought to break free.

His smile vanished, and with enough force to rattle the china inside of the cabinets behind her, Officer Sims slammed Denise's back up against them.

She gasped, as her lungs fought with the air that suddenly filled them.

After about thirty seconds of heaving she managed to speak.

"I'm sorry, Mister...what do you want?"

Hearing the defeat in her tone, the man's toothless smile returned. Upstairs, Tyson was barking madly, and Shakira could be heard crying.

"There...was that so hard?" Officer Sims asked.

Denise said nothing, but it didn't matter because he hadn't been looking for an answer.

"I need cash, woman..."

"Cash...I don't have any..."

"Hey...don't you play with me," he warned, taking a step closer.

Denise closed her eyes and swallowed.

"I'm not fucking stupid," he told her, spittle flying from his mouth in the process. "I know of the sweet little role you play for you lover. You're just as involved in the dope game as he is, and I want my cut."

Denise's eyes shot open, and she glanced at him hatefully.

"Now..." he told her.

She nodded.

"I've got some cash for you...it's over there in that closet," she said pointing. Officer Sims glanced into that direction.

"Hmm…" he said skeptically, "I hope that you don't think that I'm stupid, because I know that there's a gun over there in that closet, somewhere."

Denise didn't deny it.

"Yeah, but there's also thirteen thousand dollars in cash in that closet, as well."

Officer Sims drew his weapon and aimed it at her deliberately.

"Come on… let's go over there and get it."

Watching the crooked government official carefully, she strolled past him and crossed the room.

"You know…" he said from behind her, his weapon trained on the back of her hand, "I still owe you for pointing that huge piece that you had at me, when you were up in that window."

Denise didn't let her shock at the fact that he'd known that she'd had the drop on him earlier when he'd been talking to Curtis show. She reached the closet and placing a hand on the doorknob, she opened it slowly.

"Go…in…" he told her with a wave of his gun.

She sighed in anger and did as she was instructed. Denise could feel the deceitful cop's heavy breathing on the back of her neck. He was directly on her heels and she knew that this was his way of intimidating her. No matter how much she tried not to let him do so, it was to no avail, because she knew that there was nothing that she could do to get him out of her house, besides giving him what he came for.

She tried her best to concentrate, but Tyson's barking coming from upstairs was keeping her from doing so.

"Well…" he asked impatiently, "where is it?"

"Look …" she said snappily, peering back over her shoulder at him through the dark, "don't rush me. I can't remember where I put it."

The kitchen's lighting illuminated Officer Sims, giving the large man a menacing appearance that not only scared Denise, but would have unnerved any woman.

She both heard and saw the hammer on his revolver when he cocked it back.

"Okay…" she said aggravated beyond measure and hating the ground that the dirty cop walked on.

Kneeling, she uncovered an empty paint canister that sat in the closet's corner. Reaching inside, she found what she was in search of, and began to stand.

"Slowly…" he warned her.

Denise obliged, and turning to face him, she reached out her hand to offer Sims what she had.

In that very instant, a loud clapping sound filled the small enclosure, and a flash of light gave them both a split second of distinct visual.

The last thing that Denise saw was Officer Sims' large hand rearing back, as he raised the metallic object that he held in it. Then everything went black.

18

Thousands of feet above the Earth's surface, the winds on the Northern East coast quietly began to stir once again. The clear overhead clouds were beginning to vanish just as fast as they had materialized. The sun that had once blazed was nothing more now than a humungous sleeping eyeball. Its lid had been shut to a mere peek, and the streets of Paterson were vastly beginning to look gloomy as they had before.

Not a single drop of rain had begun to fall yet, but those that had been awake for the morning part of the day and had witnessed firsthand the aggressive winds and drenching showers earlier on, were now on high alert, anticipating the return of the brewing tropical storm that the entire state had been warned about.

The town's residents were once again moving about in an apprehensive fashion. Idle strolls turned into urgent, determined trots. Umbrellas were taken out once again, and car windows were immediately raised. Surprisingly, the owners of the retail stores that had once been shut down for business but had reopened were optimistic that the storm would pass as it had before and chose to remain open.

Klick Klak's ride home was a quiet one. He had a great deal to ponder over and was in no condition to pay any mind to the miscellaneous activities going on around him outside of his car, as he cruised through the streets of his hometown. Even a blind person couldn't have missed the telltale signs of the ensuing tropical storm that was headed their way, but in his case a tornado could have snatched him from the Earth's surface and it would have probably still taken him several minutes to realize what had happened. His mind was way too overloaded and clouded, at present.

He was on his way to do something very ruthless. He had no clue as to how he'd feel afterward, but right then the repercussions of his coming actions didn't matter. His mind was set. Something had to be done about Tommy. The dude had finally crossed the line by assaulting Jacob.

Although, it wouldn't have made any difference if it had been someone else, because if they were a part of 'One-Two Live', then they were considered to be family. That went for the women just as much as it did for the men.

Before now, they'd had minor falling outs between their rival crews, but none of their physical confrontations had taken place inside of their residing neighborhoods. It had always been on neutral turf. Tommy's brazen decision to come over to North Main and do harm to someone that was a highly regarded hustler amongst 'One-Two Live' had been a total disrespect to Klick Klak and all that he had worked hard to establish. To him, it was like having been spit in the face. There was no way that he'd let anyone get away with doing something like that.

Before he'd made his way over to the East side of town, he'd made a trip to his house, first, feeling the need to check in on Lamont. When he'd gotten there, he'd noticed that his Dodge charger wasn't in its usual parking space and had known immediately that his younger brother had taken it.

Annoyed by Lamont's absence, he'd gone inside and had gotten a much-needed necessity; something that he'd been holding onto for quite some time now, and had hurried right back out of the door. There hadn't been any need for him to hang around his house any longer than necessary, since his brother wasn't there. There was currently something more important that he had to see to, and he was afraid that if he were to sit in one place for too long, then he'd begin dwelling intensely on the subject matter and might have a change of heart. He couldn't let that happen.

Klick Klak checked his watch, and then looked at the little black box that sat on the passenger seat. He knew that the object inside of that box would get his point across clearly to

Tommy, and his entire entourage. There'd be no mistaking Klick Klak's intentions or misunderstanding his meaning behind the actions that he was about to take. He knew that if something wasn't done about what had been done to Jacob, then Tommy would assume that he'd gone soft and would come after Lamont next.

"That ain't gonna happen," Klick Klack said to no one in particular, as he drove toward his destination. He'd changed into a pair of black denim jeans and a black Champion sportswear hoodie. There was a black ski mask sitting atop of his head that he'd use when it came time for him to conceal his identity. He looked like a vicious thug that was on his way to pull off a heist.

It took him ten minutes to reach the street that Tony's barbershop was located on. He parked about twenty yards away from the establishment, hoping to go unnoticed. Allowing ten minutes to while away, he watched carefully as people came and went freely; mostly dope fiends. From what Klick Klak could see Tommy's crew didn't appear to be doing too bad. Although, the foot traffic wasn't as heavy over here as it was on the sets of the Westside, there still seemed to be enough clientele to keep food on all of the hustler's tables.

Klick Klak figured then, that Tommy was just hating on him, and being greedy for what he didn't already have. Now that he was a partial witness to how some of their operation was being run, he couldn't believe that he'd even considered going along with Tommy's girlfriend's plan to even out the stakes between the two of them .

It became obvious that she was just trying to fatten her man's pockets, and that caused a surge of anger to crawl its way into Curtis' heart. He was truly going to enjoy this.

He watched as a fiend approached a young Hispanic kid, and then stared on as the dealer made his way inside of the shop. Several seconds passed before the boy emerged with an older black man trailing behind him.

It was Tony…Tommy's second-in-command. He walked casually up to the female customer that had been waiting, and a smile crossed his lips. They embrace one another, and then began to carry on a healthy conversation.

Wondering if he'd missed something, Klick Klak strained his eyes hoping to get a better look at what was taking place. He sat back against his seat and smiled. The female that had come looking for the older gentleman wasn't a fiend…she was Tony's lady. He'd mistaken her tiny features for that of malnutrition, when really, she was just a petite woman. Now that he paid closer attention to her, he saw her striking beauty. The woman was small, but it was apparent that she was a baby doll in up-close-in-person.

Klick Klak was convinced that the woman was more than likely the mother of Tony's children.

Checking his surroundings, he reached over and picked up the little black box, before climbing out of his vehicle.

Assuming that no one was paying him any mind, he headed into the direction of where the couple stood conversing. There were still several of Tommy's hustlers standing on opposite sides of the street, but they were oblivious to the man dressed in all black that was headed their way.

Nearly ten yards from his target, Klick Klak slid his mask completely over his face, and began to open the box that he held in his hand. A couple of steps further and he stopped in his tracks. Using care, he pulled the metallic pin from the little black ball that he held.

"Aye, yo, my man!" he called out mockingly, drawing both Tony's and the girl's attention. "What's up, sucka?"

As he raised his arm and began to toss the grenade, he heard Tony's surprised expression.

"Oh, shit..." the older man exclaimed and, in a panic, he turned to flee never minding the girl.

There was a loud popping sound, and dark smoke filled the air accompanied by hundreds of tiny sparkles. Several screams came from different directions.

It took several seconds for Klick Klak to snap back to, and take off running toward his awaiting vehicles. His eyes had begun to water, and his nose stung of gunpowder, but he was sure that he could manage. He had to get away from there as fast as he could.

As he ran the last couple of yards to his vehicle, he could still see the bloody shoes that had belonged to the beautiful young lady that had been standing beside Tony, in the back of his mind. He had no clue if they had been blown off of her feet, or if her feet had been taken off along with them.

With a lot more malice than he'd known he could ever possess, he hoped with a deadly passion that the little black ball of destruction had done a lot worse damage to the man that she'd been standing with.

19

A white 2005 Chevy Impala pulled up on the North side of Montgomery Park, and sat idling for several seconds before the engine shut off. The operator of the vehicle surveyed the area carefully. He spotted what he'd been in search of and unconsciously his body tensed. His jaw flexed involuntarily, and he fought to contain his emotions.

Masking his aggravation as best as he could, he climbed out of the car and stood out in the open. Grimacing, he clutched the right side of his stomach as he stood at his full height.

"Stupid bitch…" he grumbled.

Making his way across the landscape of the park, he willed himself to remain calm, as he neared the man that sat patiently waiting for him by the basketball court. He had to be careful not to let his resentment show, because he knew that the man wasn't alone. People of his caliber were never alone. They always had someone near them; always needed to be protected from the next candidate eager to take their place.

His eyes searched the grounds as he got closer. Then, he saw them, there were four tailor-suited men spread out on all four sides of him. Each one of them were feeding breadcrumbs to eager pigeons. It was obvious that if things didn't go as planned, there'd be no escaping. Nervously, he checked his coat pocket for the package to make certain that it was still there. There was no use in him checking for his sidearm, because it'd be of no use to him under these circumstances. He'd more than likely die trying to shoot his way out of a situation.

He made it to the picnic bench and the man finally looked up at him. There was no smile. No warm greeting. He seemed unamused by Officer Sims' presence.

"Toss it on the bench table, and do it slowly," the Italian mobster told him without emotion.

Without any second thoughts, the bald cop did as he was told, then looked around cautiously. All four of the suited men were now watching him intently.

"How much is in here?"

"It's thirteen thousand," he told the corrupt councilman. "You know, that's only two thirds of what you owe us for this month, right?" Al Chino asked him.

"Yeah, Al…I know, and I'm working on getting you the rest, but…" "You ain't workin' fast enough, Sims," he warned. "You fucked up by busting my uncle's distributor during his run for mayor, and almost exposed his hand, which need I remind you would have caused him to lose the election. He gave you a second chance by allowing you to keep your life and continue workin' the streets for him. Gave you the opportunity to make up for the money that you cost him by embezzling those nigger street hustlers out there. Even lettin' you keep some of the Luciano for yourself, am I right?"

Officer Sims found the strength from deep within himself to ignore the racial comment the mobster had just made. He nodded.

"Then what the fuck's the problem?"

"Nothing… I'll get your uncle his money."

Al Chino paused, taking the moment to make certain that all of his men were still on the job. He motioned for one of them to approach.

In a matter of seconds, the man stood protectively beside him.

"Take this…" Al Chino said, handing him the clear Ziploc freezer bag full of cash that Sims had taken off of Denise, after she'd managed to shoot him in the stomach and he'd knocked her lights out. The Kevlar vest that he'd been wearing had taken most of the impact from the revolver's projectile.

"Go and get the car, Mikey," he told the obedient henchman, and obligingly the quiet gentleman headed off to do so.

Turning back to Sims, he asked,

"What about that block that I told you I wanted cleared out?"

"I'm working on it."

"Well, work faster, because I ain't got time to sit around and play fuckin' patsy all day, ya hear me! I want them off of that fuckin' block!"

Sims looked away and nodded.

"We all done here?" he asked.

"Yeah…" Al said matter-of-factly. "You can go… you just make sure that you have that other twelve thousand by the end of the week, or you're gonna have to learn how to pull a trigger with your middle finger."

Officer Sims' jaw flexed.

"Every time you come up short or late, you're gonna lose one of those digits there, buddy boy."

He watched Sims carefully, knowing that he was pissing the cop off more and more with every spoken word. He relished in that fact because he could care less. Truth was he hated darkies. If it weren't for his uncle's insistence on not killing an officer of the law, he would have been had the old coon whacked.

Sims turned and began to walk off. He was so angry at present that he could have fried an egg on his forehead. He hated having to tolerate someone talking to him in the manner that Al Chino had just done. Had it been anyone else, he would have smashed their face in until there weren't anymore teeth left inside of their head. He couldn't win that battle with those Italians, though, and he knew it. So, against everything that he ever stood for, he surrendered under their dominion and became their corrupt puppet.

With pure hatred slithering throughout his entire being, he looked back over his shoulder and caught Al Chino watching him with a look of disgust on his face.

"Yeah… I hate you too, motherfucker," he said under his breath, and kept on into the direction of his car.

Lamont sat in the driver's seat of his brother's Dodge Charger waiting patiently for Bridget to lock up the house that he had once called home. Looking back at the two-story brick house, a wave of euphoria swept over him. He couldn't help missing Mommy Sylvia, and each passing thought of her created another surge of guilt for not having come to see her sooner.

Finding Bridget here had been a blessing. Now that they were reunited and would more than likely become an item, he had something both mentally and physically satisfying to look forward to. He knew that Bridget was a person that would live up to her promises. She had said that she would be there with him throughout all of his troubles, and he believed her. She was just like him and could relate to most of what he was currently feeling.

They were one and the same, having grown up in a foster home together. There wasn't much that she didn't already know about Lamont, because since the moment that he'd been forced to move out of their home, he hadn't changed much. She was a strong, resilient young woman; possessing all of the characteristics that he needed in a lady. There was no doubt that he'd be alright with her by his side.

Exiting the house through the front door, Bridget's back was to him as she secured the locks. All of her needed necessities were already loaded up in the car, but she carried a small shoulder bag with her, as she descended the stairs and made her way toward him.

Lamont was mesmerized by her beauty . He couldn't believe how much she'd blossomed over the years. She'd somehow managed to fill-out in more ways than he could, or would have ever imagined. The eyes that he saw her through weren't those of a loving little brother. There was no way that he could ever see her that way again. The eyes that watched her carefully, now, were those of an attracted young man that had just laid eyes on his most desired damsel for the very first time. Bridget was classy, hot, and respectfully reserved. She was exactly what any man that could appreciate beauty would have loved to claim as his own.

Quickly climbing out of the car, Lamont hurried around to the other side and opened the passenger door for her.

Blushing, Bridget thanked him for his courtesy.

He kissed her cheek before shutting her inside, and rushed back around to get back in.

Sliding into his seat and securing himself inside, he crank the engine and took a quick glance at her.

She returned his stared with one of her own, and neither of them could suppress their smiles.

"You ready?" he asked.

Bridget nodded, then looked out through the windshield and up at the skyline.

"It looks like that storm is coming back, Lamont."

He followed her gaze.

"Yeah, it does, doesn't it?"

There was no way for either of them to know how much of that storm was headed their way, just as there was no way for them to know how bad the storm was that had been gradually building, back in Paterson. One thing was for certain, though, they would find out soon enough, because it was waiting on them with open arms.

Feeling more certain of himself than what he had in a very long time, Lamont put the Dodge Charger into gear and eased his way into traffic.

Together, they were on their way to weather a storm that would change their lives forever.

20

Back at the hospital, Ieisha was losing every bit of self-control that she had inside of her. It was a battle in itself for her to keep from pulling her hair out. She'd been ushered to a waiting room when the electrocardiograph machine hooked to Jacob had gone haywire, and he'd flatlined.

For three hours, now, she'd been waiting for the doctor to return with news of Jacob's condition. The last time that she'd seen him he'd been dead.

She wondered why the hospital staff was choosing to keep her in a disturbing suspense. She felt like one of the distraught family members that she'd seen in movies, and didn't know how much longer she could keep it together, because at present she was only two minutes away from becoming a total wreck.

Ieisha couldn't bear the thought of living without Jacob. If he were to die on her she was certain that she'd lose it. Just the thought of having to live under such unpleasant standards brought tears to her eyes. She'd been fighting a breakdown for too long, now.

Her tears began to flow freely and drawing her legs up to her chest where she sat on one of the cheap couches, she rocked back and forth as she choked on her sobs and fought to catch her breath.

"Why, God?" she begged to know. "Why are you taking him away from me? Please, don't take Jacob…I love him too much."

There was an elderly Caucasian woman passing by and having heard the young woman's pleas to God, she strolled over to sit beside Ieisha.

With a gentle hand, she reached out and stroked Ieisha's hair.

"Oh, honey… it's going to be alright," she soothed.

Looking over at the elderly woman whose youthful beauty still managed to show beneath her weathered skin, Ieisha could see the genuine concern in the woman's eyes, and that was all that she could take.

She collapsed into the woman's welcoming arms, and without reserve she gave into her grief entirely.

Tommy's Ford Explorer screeched to a halt at the top of his block.

"What the fuck?!" he growled, as he stared at what looked to be the scene of a horrible homicide.

There was shattered glass and a disarray of debris scattered nearly fifteen feet out into the street from where the entrance to Tony's shop had once been. Black soot covered the battered outside walls of several of the other buildings that sat next to the shop. There was crime scene tape everywhere, and the amount of police that were present was unbelievable.

From where Tommy sat, he could see SWAT, the FBI, ATF, and the DEA. All of the government officials were present on the street that he hustled on, posted up in front of his partner's spot where something terrible had obviously taken place, and it unnerved him greatly to try and think of what might have happened. Even the fire department was down there.

There was no damn way that Tommy was going to go any closer than he already was so in a hurry, he done a U-turn in the middle of the street and was about to head back the other way, but was suddenly cutoff by another vehicle.

He recognized the car immediately. It was a money-green Mercedes Benz 600, and Talil, Kwalib, Rayshawn, and Shahid all sat inside of it. It was Tony's Benz, and the owner himself sat in the backseat between Rayshawn and Kwalib. It was evident that something was terribly wrong with him, because he appeared to be unconscious and there was blood and dirt all over his clothes. Talil was driving and Shahid sat in the passenger seat. All four of them were heavily armed.

"Yo, what the fuck, y'all... what happened?" Tommy asked them nervously.

Talil spoke with urgency in his tone.

"Yo, we have to get him to a hospital somewhere out of town, son!"

"Yeah, I can see that much, but what happened?"

"Man, shit got crazy, kid," Kwalib told him from the backseat. "Nigga came from out of nowhere with a fucking grenade!"

"What?" Tommy asked not believing that he'd heard Kwalib correctly.

"Tommy, man, it was Klick Klak…we know it. But look, follow us… we are taking him to Clifton," Talil said glancing pass Tommy's truck at all of the government officials. "We'll explain everything to you once we get there. I think Tony's really fucked up, man…he's bleeding out of his ears and shit."

"Aiight…" Tommy said breathing heavily now, 'let's go."

Talil nodded and jerking the steering wheel to the right, he punched the accelerator and peeled off.

Tommy wasn't far behind them.

Curtis was frantic. He'd just performed one of the most heinous of crimes that he'd ever committed on another human being before. He'd tossed a grenade at someone for Pete's sake. He knew that war was war, but the streets of Paterson were getting to be like those of a small Middle Eastern country where hatred was plentiful. And all over some damn drug money.

Klick Klak hated the path that his life had taken, but in all honesty there was nothing that he could have done before now to change its course. He knew that, for him, hustling was his only option if he wanted to ever be wealthy enough to move up out of the ghetto. He'd tried being a standup kid, scoring A's and B's throughout grade school, but all that that had left he and his younger brother with was an empty stomach. There had been times when they'd just about had to eat raw cornmeal and ketchup sandwiches just to stay alive. Klick Klak abhorred that way of life, and his strong will and relentless drive had led him to do something about it, because being poor just wasn't for him.

In just a couple of years after being pampered by Mommy Sylvia, only to later be put out by her, Klick Klak had managed to move himself and Lamont up out of the slums. What he hadn't known, though, was that it was going to be at a huge price. Not only was his way of life about to cost him his sanity, but it was beginning to do the exact opposite of what he'd planned. Instead of creating a promising future for his bloodline, he was actually ruining the lives of those that he cared for the most.

Something had to give. He was hard pressed to get out of the game as soon as possible. It was time to take all that he'd accumulated over the years of hustling and uproot. He'd take his family somewhere further up north and settle down. Maybe even do a little bit of farming. Agriculture was known to bring in some pretty good revenue, annually.

Denise would like that, Klick Klak thought, as he tried convincing himself that it would be best for him to do something different with his life. He wanted to be able to raise Shakira without the risk of endangering her. Now that he was at war in a town where the murder rate was higher that the birthrate, it was nearly next to impossible for him to do that there.

Relocating would probably also do a good number on Lamont, and he'd probably be able to talk his brother back into the idea of attending college. It'd be a total drag for him to see Lamont's athletic abilities go to waste. The kid had worked way too hard over the years to let that happenen, and Curtis had supported him by providing him with everything that any teenage boy could ever want, or need.

Lamont should have no complaints, and that was what was involuntarily pissing Klick Klak off. His brother should have been content, but sadly that wasn't the case.

As the dark, angry clouds opened up in Passaic County, and the falling rain played like a staccato drum against Klick Klak's windshield, his mind was made up then and there. Before things got irreparably out of control, he was packing up his family and getting the hell out of dodge.

Within the next ten minutes he was pulling into Denise's driveway. He hadn't called ahead of time like he normally did, so he was relieved to find her car still sitting in its usual spot.

Exiting his vehicle, he hurried up the driveway and reached the front door in just a couple of strides. He was about to stick his key into the deadbolt lock, when he noticed that the door was slightly cracked open. All of his alarm bells went off instantly.

"What the fuck," he said, as he pushed his way inside.

He immediately picked up the sound of Tyson's loud barking that was coming from somewhere upstairs. Then he heard his daughter crying. "Denise!" he called out, while withdrawing his sidearm in one fluid motion. He waited for a fraction of a second, but no reply came. "Denise!" he called out again.

Making his way through the living room, he headed upstairs, but did so as quietly as possible. Between his daughter's wailing and Tyson's barking, his nerves were trying their best to force his concentration to falter.

Klick Klak's breathing intensified, as he got closer and closer to his daughter's bedroom. He had no idea what it was that he was about to encounter, but whatever it was he knew that it wouldn't be good. There was too much going on, now, between himself and his rivals for him to think that the war that had begun as of late wouldn't make it into the home of the ones that he cherished the most. In the ghetto, there was no such thing as honor amongst barbarians. He, himself, had just proven that several minutes ago.

The closer that he got to his daughter's room, the more on edge he became. He reached the secured door and could hear Tyson scratching vigorously at it. Bracing himself, he carefully turned the knob and shoved it open with as much force as possible, forcing Tyson to leap backward. In a stance that allowed him to pan from left to right, he scanned the room in haste, his gun hand steady and his trigger finger ready for action.

Tyson rushed him and standing on his hind legs, he greeted his second master with gratitude.

At first sight of her father, Shakira's crying ceased and pushing herself up from the spot that she'd been sitting in at the center of her room, she ran to him and wrapped herself around his legs.

"Hey, baby…" he soothed, rubbing her head with his free hand, "where's your mommy?"

She looked up at him with wide-eyes and shook her head. "Okay…" he said nervously, his eyes scanning their surroundings once more, "you don't know either."

Tyson began barking again and jumped down from where he'd been perched on Curtis' hip. Looking back up at his master, he barked one last time and then bounded out of the room. Stopping at the top of the stairs, he looked back at Klick Klak with urgency and gave a loud whine.

Getting the idea that the dog was onto something, he scooped Shakira up into one of his arms and told her, "Come on, baby, let's go find Mommy."

He followed Tyson down the stairs and became highly aware of the eerie silence inside of the entire home. His gun aimed, he moved with precaution once again.

Tyson stopped just inside of the kitchen and continued whining.

"What is it, boy?" Klick Klak asked.

The kitchen's cupboard was on the other side of the room, located near the backdoor.

The backdoor was wide-open.

Until now, he hadn't noticed the draft of air that invaded the home. There was a monthly calendar that had been hung up on the refrigerator, and it flailed in the air wildly. There appeared to be no one else inside of the room. Klick Klak's eyes searched, and once again they stopped on Tyson. He was scratching at the outside of the cupboard's door. Sticking his nose to the door's bottom , he sniffed and then began to bark wildly.

Sitting Shakira down onto her feet, Curtis told her to stay put.

Wringing her hands, she obeyed her father's order.

Klick Klak crossed the room.

Reaching the cupboard's door, he grasped the knob and braced himself.

Tyson took several steps backward to give him some room.

In one fluid motion, he twisted his wrist and snatched the door back.

Curtis' stomach dropped to his knees. His heartbeat became erratic, and his gun fell to the floor. Kneeling down, he reached a handout and felt for a pulse. A lone tear slipped from his eye, as a strong sense of relief swept over him.

"Denise..." he groaned. His baby wasn't dead...she was only unconscious.

21

The George Washington Bridge was heavy with traffic, as Lamont weaved the Dodge Charger in and out of lanes at a reasonable speed.

Inside the vehicle, music by Pop singer Rihanna played at a low volume, setting a cheerful mood despite the unpleasant weather on the outside.

Bridget, whose ride to Paterson, New Jersey felt more like an excursion was in good spirits, and did her best to influence Lamont's disposition, as well. She could see that ever since she had asked him if she could return back to Paterson with him, his confidence level had risen, and he didn't seem to be bothered by the thought of going back home as much as he had been before. It was apparent to her that he was really looking forward to her support, and in all honesty, she was looking forward to giving it to him.

The strain that was behind his eyes when he'd arrived at her house was now gone, and he was able to smile and hold a full conversation without staring off into space for seconds on end.

When he'd come to Queens and had stood on her porch, the pain on his face had made it difficult for her to recognize him. She'd been used to the youthful, vibrant Lamont that had always worn an uplifted demeanor.

The Lamont that had been so full of life and could turn anyone else's sour mood into a soul full of sugar was the person that she remembered. He'd been her sweetener on so many different occasions when they'd been younger, that it was a wonder that he hadn't sensed her emotional attachment to him way back then. Bridget had clearly worn her feelings for him on her sleeve.

The good thing about it all was he knew, now. There was no more confusion between the two of them. She knew that she'd missed and loved him, and there was no doubt in her mind that he felt the same way about her.

Turning in her seat toward Lamont, Bridget reached over and took his free hand into hers. She raised it to her lips and kissed it gently.

The sweet gesture brought a smile to Lamont's lips, and he glanced over at her. At the sight of her beauty he was forced to take a deep breath before he spoke. It had been so long since he had seen Bridget's face, and it was a bit of a shock to see how lovely she'd become over the years. When they were younger, she'd been pretty, but the way that she looked now was beyond pleasing.

"What's up, baby...you okay?""Lamont, I don't think that I've ever been better," she told him, "I've waited for this day to come for so long that you'd not believe what I'm feeling right now, even if I could explain it to you."

"Bridget, did you really miss me that much?"

"Oh, God, yes, Lamont, you have absolutely no idea," she told him.

Lamont directed his eyes back toward the traffic.

"Bridget, I'm gonna be honest with you…I hadn't realized just how much I've been missing you, until the moment that you called my name from up on that porch and I recognized who you were," he admitted. "I wonder, now, why it took me so long to get the notion to return to Queens. I should have been coming back to at least see mommy Sylvia." His last words were said with conviction.

She reached over and stroked the side of his face.

"Lamont don't blame yourself for not coming back sooner. Mommy Sylvia knew that you still loved her…even Curtis. She never stopped loving either of you, and she used to talk about you all of the time. As far as it goes for me…" Bridget shrugged, "we were young, and at the time we were considered to be brother and sister. You could have never known that I was in love with you, because I was too afraid to tell you. Not only that, but I didn't even realize that I was in love, myself. I just knew that I never wanted to lose you."

Lamont nodded letting her know that he understood entirely.

"So…you're really going to keep me in your life from here on out?"

He asked.

"What…" Bridget asked, "are you serious? Do you think that I'm going to let you out of my sight? No way; not gonna to happen. I'm gonna to stick to you like glue, buddy, until I know that you're never going to step out of my life again."

"Word?" he asked chuckling, feigning surprise.

"Oh, you don't believe me, huh?" she asked sassily, while rolling her neck as though she were ready to tell him off.

"Nah, Bridget, it ain't like that. I believe you, ma. I was just playing with you."

"Yeah, okay…" she said smiling, and happy to see him back in better spirits. "I was about to go all sister on you."

"Yeah, I could see that…" he said laughing, "cause all that pretty white skin started turnin' fire-red."

"Oh, hush, Lamont…" Bridget said playfully, and pulled his hand up to her lips once again.

She gazed out through the windshield and stared up at the sky. What she saw there concerned her.

"Lamont, the weather seems to be getting pretty bad, doesn't it?"

He stole a glance up toward the sky as well, and his smile faded.

"Yeah, it does ," he agreed.

"I hope that it passes over," she told him, and he could hear the nervousness in her voice.

Out of nowhere, chills ran down the center of his back, causing him to shiver slightly.

"Bridget, me   too. The weather report said something about a hurricane."

"I'm not sure that a storm like that could occur in these northern states, Lamont... are you?" she asked.

"Nah, baby, I don't think so, either" he told her, but his answer hadn't sounded too convincing.

Up on the George Washington, the winds whipped around the car like insane ghosts demanding to be noticed. It had nearly become a battle for Lamont to keep the Charger aligned in its own lane.

As they drove, they were unable to see out over the side of the bridge and down into the river. Had they been, they would have really become unnerved, because ever since the rain had gone from a drizzle to an all-out downpour, the waters had been rising several feet every hour, and could now be seen creeping up onto the edges of the land's soil.

It would be several more hours before the real effects of the storm would reveal themselves. No one could possibly prepare themselves for what was to come. Some things could be approached with precaution. Some things could simply be avoided entirely, whereas other were just inescapable.

Fate had its own way of being undeniable. What fate wanted, fate went after, and whatsoever fate desired, it conquered. It was just as simple as that.

On this day, fate became its own entity, and took on its own name; a name that would be documented in history. A name that would become monumental, but not because of the pleasantries that it brought to man. The name that fate would adhere to would become historical only because of its ability to possess such a genteel moniker, yet in the same breath deliver so much destruction to the lives of millions of people that it would never be forgotten.

By the time that Irene hit inland, it would be far too late to avoid, because both Lamont and Bridget would be back in Paterson.

Both the Ford Explorer and the Mercedes Benz that belonged to the members of the 'D-pound Crew' screeched to a halt not far from the city of Clifton's hospital's emergency room entrance. Kwalib and Rayshawn scrambled out of the luxury car first, and Talil and Shaid followed behind. In a scurry, all four men moved with urgency, as they worked to pull Tony from the backseat of the car without causing him any further injury. The middle-age man had yet to gain consciousness.

From where Tommy still sat behind the wheel of his truck, he watched in shock as the four men hastily removed his friend and attempted to carry him inside. He hadn't had much of a chance to assess the degree of Tony's injuries. Now that he had a clear view of him, it was apparent that the man was in very bad shape because he was covered in blood from his head to his feet.

His limbs dangled loosely, as the men toted him off. His clothes looked as though the man had tried to sprint through a blazing furnace.

They were forced to allow Tony's head to lull as they struggled to move him, and Tommy could see that there was a large patch of hair and a reasonable amount of skin missing from his friend's skull.

The sight of it brought a vile taste of fear to the back of his throat. Never before had he seen such destruction caused until today. It was unnerving to know that the level of feuding between the rivaling groups had actually escalated to such heights. Tommy had done some barbaric things in the past, but what had occurred on his block twice today had been outright heinous.

First the boy, and now Tony. Yet, neither of them was able to cause the amount of grief that the death of his sister had.

It was said that when one person died, two more would follow. Death came in threes.

Today that saying rang true, Tommy thought.

From the look of Tony as he was being carried off and rushed into the emergency room, Tommy was certain that his crime partner would be the third amongst his family to die that day, and it angered him beyond reason.

He was not going to just lie down and accept defeat because things were beginning to look unnervingly dangerous. Death was no longer a concern of his, because it was obvious now that it was unavoidable. He most certainly wasn't going to let his sister's death go unavenged. Somebody was going to pay for Alaena's life with their own. And if the myth about people dying in threes was true, then someone other than Curtis' little brother would be meeting their maker soon, as well.

Tommy was done playing around. The war that he was fighting had just been declared a code red. Anything or anyone that got in his way from then on out was considered to be fair game. He couldn't sit around and wait for his enemy to come to him inside of his own territory again. He was going to meet his enemy head on.

There was nothing that he could do for Tony at present, anyhow, besides go and find the coward that did this to him. Maybe… just maybe he'd be able to get rid of Curtis before he took care of his little brother.

Tommy waited for all four of his men that were carrying Tony to disappear inside, before he whipped his truck around and peeled out of the parking lot. He eased his way back into traffic, and without looking back, he floored the accelerator and headed back toward the city of Paterson.

22

The room was dark, and the air inside of it was cool against her skin. All of the sounds that surrounded her were alien, but the smells that invaded her senses were very familiar.

Her head felt congested, and there was an aching pressure that felt like someone was strumming each and every nerve-ending inside of her face, accompanied by a dull thumping at the back of her skull. She felt nauseated; like she was on the verge of vomiting.

At first, there were no other feelings in her body. She had no idea that she lay unmoving on her living room couch in the arms of her protector. There was no indication that there was anything out of the ordinary going on with her physical disposition at present. She merely suspected that she was suffering from some sort of severe sinus headache, or something of that nature. Her assumptions were efficient, that is, until Denise moved. Then everything came to life.

Her right leg twitched, and she raised her knee. Both of her hands balled at her sides, and then unclenched. Her head rolled from side to side, and her mouth opened as though she were about to speak.

She was parched and began to cough.

The darkness that had surrounded her slowly turned into an unfamiliar disarray of lights. That's when she realized that her eyes had been closed. Still, though, her vision remained blurry for several more seconds, and willing her eyes to adjust only caused an increase in the thumping inside of her skull.

She rolled her tongue around inside of her mouth, and somehow found the ability to groan.

There were strange sounds coming from somewhere in the background and the irregularity of them disturbed Denise, causing the hair on her forearms to stand on end.

She raised her hands and rubbed irritably at her eyes. Waiting patiently, all of the different figures and colors came together in front of her. Relief swept over her. She finally knew what the alluring fragrance that she'd been smelling was.

It was Curtis and she was lying with her head in his lap.

"Hey, baby..." he greeted her, while gently caressing the side of her face. His jaw was set, and his expression was stern. He'd been worrying over her for the past hour. "How do you feel?"

Denise let out another groan, before she spoke.

"Curtis, I feel like somebody smacked me across the head with a baseball bat."

She watched as the muscles in his jaw flexed. The frown on his face was deep, and he looked as if he were undecided about something.

"You look like someone smacked you across the head with a baseball bat…right on top of your forehead."

"Huh?" Denise asked, and raised a hand to get a feel of what Curtis was referring to.

"Unh uh," he said, catching her hand in mid-air, "I've got you bandaged up, and you don't need to be bothering it right now."

"Bothering what?" she asked with concern.

"There's a gash…" Curtis told her, "a deep one."

"Oh, my God," she said, willing herself not to panic, and she instinctively reached for the bandage again, although, this time she stopped herself.

"Denise, baby, what happened?" he asked her.

She moved to sit up, and with as much gentleness as he could muster, he helped her do so.

Her head began to spin, so she paused and waited for the nausea to pass. Finally, she was able to look Curtis in his eyes.

"Baby, how long have I been out?"

He reached for her and pulled her closer, so that she could rest her head against his chest.

"I don't know, Denise. When I got here I… I found you already unconscious…lying inside of the kitchen cupboard."

Denise closed her eyes, as short flashes of what had taken place between her and the crooked cop played over in her mind. She cringed when she remembered that the officer had hit her in the face with something hard. She'd shot the bastard, yet he'd somehow still managed to knock her unconscious.

"Well, how long have you been here with me?"

"Just over an hour," he told her.

She pulled back from him with a start and glared at him.

"Curtis, the money…"

"It's gone," he told her.

"Damn it…" she said angrily, making an attempt to pull away from him, but he wouldn't allow it.

"That was my emergency money."

"Doesn't matter, baby, it was only thirteen stacks, right?" She said nothing. She only frowned and stared past him. "Hey, you hear me? That was chump change…ain't no need to stress over that shit," he said with irritation. "I'm just glad that you're okay."

She thought about something and that brought her gaze back up to his face.

"Curtis, where's Shakira?"

"She and Tyson are next door at the neighbor's, until I figure out what in the hell is going on?"

She sighed in relief, knowing that their child was in safe hands. The man that lived next door to them with his wife and children was an active marine, and she and Curtis were good friends with him. He'd protect Shakira with his life.

"What happened, Denise? Who did this to you?"

She didn't know if she should tell him or not, because she knew that once she did more trouble would ensue. Yet, she knew that it would be dangerous to keep it from him. He had to know that that crooked cop had returned to her home and had robbed her.

"Curtis..." she paused, "you remember that cop that you were talking to in the backyard, earlier today?"

Denise watched him carefully, and she could already see his anger taking on a life of its own.

"Yeah...what about him?" he asked in a restrained tone.

"Curtis, he came back and..." she didn't get to finish, because he shoved her off of him and was on his feet in a flash.

"What are you saying, Denise...that that motherfucker came by here while I was gone, and you let him in? Did he do this to you?" he asked heatedly.

"Yes, Curtis, he did do this to me, but I didn't let him in."

"Then how'd he get in?!"

"He fucking broke in, how do you think!" she said with exasperation.

"What happened, Denise? Tell me what happened. What'd he say he came back for?"

"Money...money, Curtis, he wanted money. He said that he came for money and that we should be more hospitable toward him."

Curtis' hands balled into fists at his sides. He'd been pacing back and forth while listening to her explain what had happened, but he now stood motionless.

For the first time since Denise had awakened, she was able to pay close attention to the horrific sounds of the weather outside. The winds were howling like a thousand misplaced souls in search of an eternity of peaceful sleep that would never come. There was rain pelting the exterior of the house like tiny bullets being fired from a Gatling gun.

She stole a glance out of one of the living room windows and could see the large elm trees swaying as though they were drunken by the mass amount of precipitation.

She shivered and looked back to Curtis. Her eyes grew wide at the sight of him. She hadn't taken her eyes off of him for that long, yet he'd somehow managed to withdraw a pair of identical handguns that he'd been concealing.

He was looking down at the floor when he spoke.

"That's it...I can't take any more of that motherfucka's shit. It's over for him. He's a crooked ass cop, and if nobody else will get rid of the piece of shit, then I will."

"Curtis, no… please, don't go out there and do anything crazy," she begged, and in three quick strides she was back in arms- reach of him.

She placed a hand on his chest, and reached behind his neck with her other, pulling his face downward for a kiss.

He allowed her to caress his lips with her own but refused to return the show of affection.

Curtis' mind was made up, and there was nothing that could change it. There was no way in hell that he was going to allow what officer Sims had done to go unpunished. The man had broken into the home of his only child and her mother, and had assaulted the love his life and had robbed her. Officer Sims was a savage and deserved to be treated like one.

Denise looked up into Curtis' eyes, and there was no mistaking what she saw there…pure hatred for a man that had harmed her and had threatened her life. He had broken into the home of a kingpin's first lady and had taken what he'd wanted.

It was the will to kill in cold blood that she saw in her man's eyes, and a harsh sense of reality swept through the room, forcing her to accept what she knew that she could not prevent. There was no stopping Curtis from going out and hunting down the Passaic County police officer that didn't deserve to wear a badge.

"Go upstairs and pack some things for you and Shakira," he said sternly, his voice as cold as the hail that had just begun to fall. "Y'all are going to stay with the neighbors, until I get back."

"Curtis, please, baby don't…"

There was no use. He turned on his heel and left her standing there alone inside of the living room.

There was something that he needed to do before he went after the dirty cop.

23

A black 2010 Maserati sat idling on the corner of 17th and Park Avenue, it was dark tinted windows concealing the identity of its occupants. There were three men inside, one driver, one gunman, and the person whose interests lie in the setting before them. Two men sat up front-one in the back. The two up front were there solely for the purpose of protecting the man in the backseat, their boss.

A man of both political business affairs and underground criminally organized activities, Al Chino was widely known for his low level of tolerance for those who either knowingly or unknowingly deferred his efforts at attaining something that he wanted badly. Not only that, but he hated it whenever someone disobeyed an order that he'd given.

From where he sat, he didn't know exactly what category the situation before him lie in, but he knew that one thing was for certain… he was pissed.

There were government officials from nearly every judicial branch rambling about on the block that he and several other councilmen had their sights set on. It appeared that something very destructive had taken place in the area, and that someone had been heinously murdered. The blood splatters that had once been visible, though, were now non-existent due to the massive rainfall, but there was crime scene tape and debris everywhere. It was apparent that some sort of weapon of mass destruction had been used. A weapon that on most occasions would have been next to impossible for any normal citizens to attain. And although there were some heavily paid drug dealers in Paterson, Al Chino doubted that they'd have the covert connections to acquire any number of explosives that weren't homemade.

Figuring in those factors, he came to the conclusion that there was only one person that could have possibly possessed that degree of clout…veteran police officer Lionel Sims.

The piece of shit had obviously grown impatient with the corner hustlers, and had idiotically chosen to resort to drastic measures. Now the fucking FBI, ATF, DEA, Task Force, and Bomb Squad were all at the same location, at the exact same time. Of course, there were Paterson Police on the scene as well, yet Officer Sims was nowhere in sight.

It was apparent that they'd been out there for quite some time, now, because there were detainees sitting in the back of several of the patrol vehicles, and the officials were readying to leave.

It was a monstrous scene that they were leaving behind, one that would more than likely make the newspaper's front-page headlines, along with the morning news. It would be news that would do the city of Paterson's new mayor's image no good whatsoever. Such violence in a town that was already on the brink of causing the state of New Jersey to have to declare a state of emergency was diminishing to one's authoritative characterization.

Because of what had taken place, Al Chino's uncle would be made to look like a political figure that was unable to govern the streets of his own city. He'd be made to look just as some white-collar politics had already deemed him; a rookie; the weak link to a city that was already teetering on the brink of ruin.

There was no way that the person that had caused this amount of destruction should get away with what they had done. They needed to be punished...had to be. And though the culprit's actions would be brought to justice, the hand that he would be punished by would not be that of the town's judiciaries. Their system would be way too lenient on one of their own, even if they did set him up by creating their own solid evidence to hold against him. Officer Sims wasn't a man that should be punished like an officer of the law. He wasn't your typical everyday cop. He was a monster when he wanted to be. A coldblooded animal. There was only one way that he'd be able to understand the severity of the stupid mistake that he'd made. There was only one way that he'd come to the realization of his errors in his last few minutes of a life that he didn't deserve. In order to chastise an animal-make him aware of the wrong that he'd done, and assure that he'd never see the opportunity to make the same mistake twice in his life-you had to use that culprit's exact same kind of characteristics against him.

If you wanted an animal to feel punished, then you had to use another animal to punish him.

"Let's go," Al Chino told his driver, and quietly the Maserati pulled away from the curb.

Curtis pulled into his driveway and hopped out of his vehicle with breakneck speed. He was in a hurry to find out if Lamont had returned back home, yet, so that he could move onto the next issue at hand that had somehow found its way amongst the collage of unprecedented trials that were already troubling his life. He couldn't stand to think that something else might come bull rushing at him anytime soon. He honestly didn't know how much more of it all he could take, before he lost control of his rational decision making and began coming up with irresponsible impromptu resolutions like the one that he'd just implemented.

The incident over on the Eastside in Tommy's territory couldn't have been avoided. What those guys had done to Jacob had been totally uncalled for, and ruthless.

Tommy and his boys were now playing a game that Klick Klak refused to let them win. They were crossing over into a lane that they were by far unprepared for, because there was no way that they were equipped with enough weaponry to equalize the battlegrounds between themselves and Klick Klak's crew. Or at least that was what Curtis believed.

'One-Two Live' was too deep in active members...way too deep for someone with a crew as small as Tommy's to think that they could overrun the Westside. It should have been evident enough that they weren't prepared to take on Curtis' crew, because he'd yet to involve any of his affiliates, and had still been able to cause Tommy's entourage enough grief to the point that they'd have nightmares for the next few years to come. The 'D-Pound' would lose this war, and Curtis was sure of it.

That wasn't the issue that was troubling him, as much as it was the matter of dealing with a dirty cop. Officer Sims was a fucking problem, one that would surely be dealt with. He was the worst of the worst, an old money hungry black bastard. He didn't seem to know when to quit. His only motive was to attain money by way of extortion. He cared not that the person that he was taking it from had acquired it illegally. He only wanted what wasn't his, what he hadn't had to sweat and hustle for. He wanted to rape other people, and strip them of their blood-money. Money that some people had gone to jail for. Money that others had died for and money that in the end, he would die for. And just as Klick Klak would see to the demise of Tommy and his crew, so would he deliver the exact same fate to the corrupt government official.

Oblivious of the fact that his Dodge Challenger had yet to return, he sprinted toward the house.

The icy rain tore at his face, and the wind whipped around him like an extraterrestrial maddened spirit trying desperately to abstract him from the Earth's surface. Fighting against nature, he reached his front porch and slipped his house key into the bolt lock. It took him a couple of seconds before he finally made his way inside.

The house was quiet, other than the disturbing sounds of the storm outside. Curtis headed through the living room and found his way inside of the kitchen. It was just as desolate as the last room.

"Lamont!" he called out and waited for a response. When none came, he made his way to the backdoor and checked to see if it was still locked. It was.

"Lamont!" he called out again, as he made his way for the stairs that would take him up to his brother's bedroom.

Taking them two at a time, Curtis reached the top and in several more strides he was standing outside of his brother's bedroom door. He placed his ear to it and listened.

There was an odd noise coming from the other side, and it piqued his curiosity. On any other occasion, he would have assumed that

Lamont was either asleep, or didn't quite feel like being bothered for the time being. Under those circumstances he would have left his brother be. But with all that was going on Curtis wasn't willing to allow his brother that luxury, so without giving it much thought, he opened the door and stepped inside of the room.

He was immediately taken aback by the setting before him. Lamont's room was in a total mess, and there was a window not far from the bed that sat wide-open, allowing a very large amount of rain to enter and soak up the carpet.

Yet, there was no sign of his brother.

"Damn it..." Curtis said with annoyance. He crossed the room in a hurry and closed the window. The plush carpet felt soggy beneath his feet, and he wondered what sense it would have made for his brother to leave the window open, knowing that there was a storm coming.

"Where in the hell are you, Lamont?" he asked out loud. Turning so that he could take a better survey of the mess, it took Curtis only a couple of seconds to notice something that became very alarming. Lamont's room wasn't just in disarray from the lack of his brother cleaning it. His room was a disaster because it had been deliberately ransacked. It appeared that someone had been looking for something, and not just any something. They'd been looking for something of value, which explained why Lamont's window had been left open. Whoever it was had been in a rush to find whatever they were in search of and had gotten the hell out of there before they got caught. It wasn't hard to figure out what they'd been looking for either...money. The question was who would have known that Lamont had a nice stash of cash put up somewhere, or even where he lived, for that matter, because Curtis didn't allow just anyone to visit their home.

At that very second, it hit him... Officer Sims. He was the only one that knew just about all that there was to know about both Lamont, and Curtis.

"Shit..." he said angrily, as he stormed out of the room and headed for his own, "Lamont, where in the fuck are you, boy?"

Entering his bedroom, he headed straight over to the walk-in closet. Sliding its mirrored door back, he pushed a hefty amount of hanging clothes to the side, and gained access to a three-foot-tall, two foot wide safe that had been bolted down to the floor.

Kneeling down, he punched in a six-digit code and the safe's door unlatched with a hiss. With a sigh, he took out every piece of artillery that he thought he might need, including his Kevlar vest.

Officer David Sims was in a hurry. He had just broken into another civilian's home, albeit a drug dealer's, but the law was the law, and yet again he'd found himself acting as a criminal. He'd just climbed into the window of a seventeen-year-old boy's room and had robbed him of what was probably the kid's only savings. Thirty-five hundred dollars of someone else' money now sat snugly inside of his jacket's pocket. Assuming that the cash had been attained by way of illegal drug activity, he tried convincing himself that there was actually no harm done. Attaining something illegally from someone that had gained it illegally was not a crime in his eyes. He was only taking what was owed to the government. It wouldn't be missed. The kid would probably just sell more bricks of heroin and get it all back without any problem. Who's to say that if he hadn't of broken into that house that someone else wouldn't have after the storm had come and gone, because from the looks of things one was surely coming. A bad one, too. The weatherman had called it Irene. People were known to start looting in desperation after a storm.

As he drove, he wondered why someone would even give a disastrous storm such a serene epithet that was meant for an entity whose characteristics consisted of love, and peace. Irene was a woman's name, and man's counterpart didn't cause total destruction unless they were completely incompetent and void of their God-given compassion, as the storm that was headed their way would be. Only the acts of the human male could instill total fear in the toughest of both man and womankind. It was like the meteorologists had wanted to play some kind of a cruel joke on the people of New Jersey. The way that he'd spoken of Hurricane Irene with the sickening tone of affection in his voice as if he were in love was troubling.

America was sick, and Officer Sims knew that he'd contracted its moral-eating virus. Since he'd fallen to the evils of his job, he'd lost his way and had become demoralized just as the masses had. He was now amongst the populace of the failures that he detested. He was one of them, one of the criminals. That is what was the most demeaning to him. He hated the feeling of relation between himself, and those that were supposed to be on a lesser level of society, which had been constructed to conform to people such as himself, not those that he'd sworn to take down.

Somewhere along the way, all of that had changed and he no longer fit within the classification of his own kind. Society had turned its nose up at him. He'd become an anti-social. He was now what he hated, and he blamed it all on those pieces of shit drug dealers, and fake-ass politicians that were actually members of the mafia. If it hadn't of been for them and their obtuse alliance with some dope pushing street punks, then he wouldn't be in the unsatisfying position that he was currently in. If he had never had to bust that dealer that had been working illegally for Al Chino's uncle, whom was now the mayor of Passaic County, then he would never have become indebted to the heartless mobsters. It wasn't his fault…they were the criminals. They were the ones that had been cheating at the game of life; not him.

Sims' stomach churned and the muscles in his forearms flexed, as he gripped the steering wheel of his unmarked vehicle. He was so mentally distracted at present that he had no idea whether or not if he were hungry, or just plain sick to his stomach from the way that he'd been living his life as of late. For nearly three decades he'd been in total control of his career. He'd been the one applying the pressure to those that he felt deserved it. Now, after one faulty misstep, he was the one being pressured, and the realization of his vulnerability under the hands of another man was the one thing that he just couldn't stand.

Sims made up his mind then and there that he was tired of being pushed around by those dickless mafia impersonators. He was going to pay them this one last time and that was it. He wasn't going to allow them to continue to extort him any longer. There wasn't going to be anymore monthly or weekly payments. This was it; they weren't getting shit else from him. Those bastards didn't know who they were dealing with. It was time to show them. No fat-faced Italian punk was going to tell him when and where to piss. When he got ready to piss, he was going to do so wherever and whenever he pleased and at present he wanted nothing more than to piss on them…the mobsters in the expensive suits.

He'd show Al Chino and his weak ass goons who they were dealing with; a man that had once been a vicious police officer known entirely for his brutal tactics. He was a predator, not the prey and he refused to let anyone prey on him. Currently, he was surprised at himself for having let things get this far with the mobsters. They were in for a rude awakening, because their reign over the city of Paterson was about to come to an abrupt end. Sims was going to take his city back, even if it meant that innocent blood had to shed in order for him to do so. He'd make certain that Al Chino's uncle's term as mayor came to an early halt. He would expose them for the criminals that they were, and in the end, when everything was back to the way that it had been before those Sicilian's had invaded the state of New Jersey and tainted the streets of Paterson with their ways, he'd run for mayor and get all things back in order.

Sims grinned mischievously as he drove, and his grip loosened on the steering wheel as he began to relax. He'd come up with a plan; a solution to all of his problems, and it was one that he would make sure to put into action. There was nothing or no one that was going to stand in his way…not even Hurricane Irene.

The storm seemed to progress with every passing second. The rain came down, now, like an angry icy waterfall, causing Officer Sims to have to slow down in order to maintain a reasonable visual of the road passing beneath him. The winds had picked up dramatically, and he wondered if the pull in the steering wheel that he was feeling was because of it. If so, then he figured that it had to be up to about eighty miles per hour, by now. It was evident that the storm was reaching its advanced stages. Seeking shelter would have been the wisest thing to do, but there was one more heist that he had to pull off, before he could do so. One more raid and he'd be able to payoff Al Chino for the very last time.

Reaching a four-way intersection on the Westside of town, he slowed and came to a complete stop sign. Using precaution, he looked both ways before proceeding any further, although, he doubted that there would be much traffic under the current weather conditions. Halfway across the intersection he caught a glimpse of something out of the corner of his eye, but by the time that he turned his head to see what it was, it was too late.

The 2012 Durango rammed into the side of his vehicle with so much force that the side that it had been hit on rose several feet off the ground, and the entire car slid nearly fifteen feet on its two wheels, before it finally toppled over, holding Officer Sims prisoner. The side that had been hit appeared to be smashed in completely. Had there been any passengers they would have surely been killed on impact.

The front end of the Durango had sustained some damage, but not as much as the vehicle that it had run into. The truck's engine sputtered and smoke seeped out from under the hood.

Slowly, the driver climbed out of the SUV and examined the damage to the vehicles. With a quick survey, he determined that it wasn't all that bad, although, it wouldn't have mattered if it had been because he'd never drive the truck again anyhow. It was a rental; a throwaway and had only been purchase for the purpose of completing a job; this job.

The rain fell in a tumultuous downpour all around him. The expensive black leather attire that he wore, including the gator-skin boots that dressed his feet made him entirely repellant to the weather. There was a hood partially covering his head and concealing his face. Slowly and deliberately, he made his way across the street heading into the unmarked car's direction.

With every step that he took, the water splashed beneath him. His gait was that of a trained professional. In just a matter of seconds, he was standing in front of him.

The man dressed in black crouched down in front of Officer Sims and that caught the restrained cop's attention. Immediately becoming nervous, he stopped what he was doing and stared at the hooded man.

"Hey… man, help me out of here!" he told the mysterious person with irritation.

For several seconds the man neither did, nor said anything; his face hidden from Sims' view. Then, with a languid swipe of his hand, he removed his hoodie, revealing his face to the unfortunately doomed man that he'd been paid handsomely to find and murder on this stormy day.

Officer Sims' eyes turned into slits, as he studied the man carefully. He was an African American, just as he.

"Please, brother…help me out," he pleaded in a stern tone.

The black man with salt and peppered hair shook his head, and with the same hand that he'd removed his hoodie with, he reached beneath his coat and withdrew a nickel plated .45caliber pistol with a six inch suppressor attached to it.

Without further ado, Officer Sims knew exactly why the man was there. "Shit…" he swore with panic, "come on…tell Al Chino that I'm going to pay him his fucking money!"

The man's gun hand rose, and he aimed the pistol directly at Sims' chest.

"Hey…you don't have to do this!" Sims tried reasoning, but the man still would not speak.

He watched as the man's finger slid over the trigger.

"Damn it, you bastard, I've got a wife!"

There was a slight flicker in the man's eyes, but just as soon as it had appeared, it vanished. "At least tell me your fucking name! I don't want to be whacked by a fucking nobody. What's your damn name?!" he pleaded.

"That's an honorable question," the man said finally speaking. His voice was unnervingly calm, just as that of a trained assassin should have been. He was nothing like the two prude characters that had played the roles of hired gunmen in the motion picture Pulp Fiction.

"My name's Terrance, but, most people just call me Mr. Duncan." And without any more words being spoken, he squeezed the trigger and sent Officer Sims onto his eternal resting place. Once...twice... then a third for good measure.

24

Lamont and Bridget made it into Paterson just as the storm began to progress. Hail the size of mothballs pattered against the windshield of the Charger in a steady rhythm, yet they were way too embellished in their conversation to pay the inclement weather any mind.

Having the chance to catch up on old times was beginning to feel like a high that they just couldn't get enough of. Who would have thought that they'd be reunited at a time like this? It wasn't a blessing that they had even asked for, but one that they greatly appreciated. Neither of them would have traded in their reunion for anything else. Both their pleasures lay solely in their determination to never be separated again, no matter what.

Lamont knew that Bridget was what he needed in his life. She was the element that he'd been missing. In her presence, he felt complete. She was his excitement, his edge, his strong sense of spontaneity that he'd been in search of during his boring school days. With her around he wouldn't need to become a part of the streets just to feel in tune with the untamed part of the world, because most didn't know it, but there was a wild side to Bridget that could keep any young man like himself busy for days on end.

She was just the type of girl that someone who was about to graduate from high school needed.

Bridget was a well-grounded young woman. She was educated, hardworking, and very responsible. On top of that, she was also very affectionate and caring. Until now, Lamont hadn't realized how much he'd missed those characteristics being showered on him. There was also the fact that she was and always had been one of the most beautiful females that he'd ever laid eyes on. Now she was his to claim.

Reaching for her hand, Lamont asked, "So, Bridget, how are we going to work this out? Am I going to have to move back to Queens to be with you, or are you going to come and stay with me in Paterson?"

"I don't know, Lamont," she told him, while stroking his hand and watching his profile. "What do you want to do?"

"Well, as you know, I'm graduating this year and Curtis expects me to go off to college. He thinks that I should accept one of the scholarships that have been offered to me, and that I should go off to play ball, instead of staying close to Paterson."

Her mouth skewered as she contemplated that idea.

"I don't know, Lamont that might not be a bad idea."

He looked at her as if she were out of her mind.

"And what about us? I mean, I hadn't planned on leaving   Paterson before, but I really know, now, that I'm not going anywhere far off? I'm not trying to be away from you anymore, Bridget." "Yes, Lamont, I feel the same way, but if we had to do that then I'm sure that we could make a long-distance relationship work until you graduated."

"No..." he said shaking his head and directing his attention back to the road. His visual of the street passing beneath them was beginning to become badly obstructed, so he slowed down considerably, despite the fact that there weren't many other travelers out.

Bridget sighed in resignation, but her grip on Lamont's hand tightened.

"Lamont, I know...I don't really want to be away from you any longer than I have to ever again, either, but if you asked me to... or needed me to, I'd give you a hundred and ten percent of my love and support."

He glanced at her again.

"Damn, baby, you're making me fall in love with you."

"I thought that you were already in love with me, Lamont Crowder?"

"Bridget, you know that I've always loved you, but... this is new. I didn't know that I loved you like this."

She smiled.

"I know what you mean. I was only kidding with you."

A short silence passed between them.

"How do you think Curtis will react when he sees me?" she asked Lamont. The question had been at the back of her mind since the moment that she'd agreed to return back to Paterson with him.

"Oh, probably just as I did when I showed up at Mommy Sylvia's house and you answered the door. He'll be in total shock."

"You don't think that he'll be upset once he sees me, do you?" she asked seriously.

"What…hell no… why would he bad mad at you?" Lamont asked confused.

"Well, you know, Mommy Sylvia did put y'all out, and continued to raise me afterward. He might resent me for that," she told him seriously.

"No, Bridget, Curtis is not like that. He's never been upset with Mommy Sylvia for putting us out, because he knew that she was right, and she had a legitimate reason to. She had other children to raise, and she didn't want him corrupting them…like he did me."

"Okay, if he won't be upset about any of that, then what about when he finds out about us?" she asked.

"What about us?" Lamont asked.

"We used to be brother and sister, Lamont. He might find something wrong with us being together."

"We were foster siblings, Bridget, not real brother and sister. Besides, if he doesn't like it, too bad. I'm not losing you to anything, or anyone else. He was the reason why we got separated in the first place, and I refuse to let him do that to us again."

She studied his facial expression and knew without a doubt that he was serious. It made her heart flutter and her stomach feel as if she had a thousand butterflies flying around inside of it. Lamont really did love her. "You know..." she said with a smile, "there's a junior college not far from the house in Queens, and I hear that they have a pretty good football team."

Lamont grinned at her devilishly.

"Word... that's what's up. I'm moving back to Queens, then," he told her.

Bringing his hand up to her lips, Bridget kissed it and the joy inside of her showed. Her eyes glowed with amusement, as they stared at one another for several seconds.

With a sigh of satisfaction and relief, Bridget's gaze returned back to the road... then her eyes grew wide.

"Lamont, watch out!" she screamed, but it was too late. They smashed into the vehicle that had been sitting propped up on its side in the middle of the road, and the impact sent them careening into an eight-foot-deep ditch.

Back at the hospital, Ieisha paced impatiently inside of the waiting room that she'd not left for the past several hours. She'd been stressfully wringing her hands so much that they were beginning to hurt, although she couldn't help it. She had to do something to keep from going insane.

Since the doctors had rushed her out of Jacob's room, they'd not been back to give her an update on the status of her fiancé's health. She had no clue as to whether or not if Jacob was still alive or if he had passed. The last time that she had seen him he'd been dead, and had been lying lifelessly on his bed while they had frantically begun to work on him.

Before they'd rushed her out of the room, Ieisha had gotten a chance to witness the abrupt stop of his labored breathing. One second his chest had been rising and falling, and the next it had just gone completely still. The sight of it had taken her breath away, and she'd nearly fainted. She wanted to pray, now, but the last time that she had been doing so Jacob had died on her. She didn't know whether or not if they'd been able to revive him, but if they had then she didn't want that to happen again. She was both afraid and confused.

She couldn't lose Jacob, she loved him way too much. She didn't think that she could go on living life without him.

Ieisha realized that this was exactly one of the reasons why people say that being in love is both a gift and a curse.

As she paced nervously back and forth, she cursed the doctors for not having returned to deliver any type of news of Jacob's health. She thought of how cruel it was to keep a person waiting in suspense, as they were her. All she wanted to know was if her man was going to be alright.

"Please, Jacob..." she said breaking the silence in the room, "fight, baby. Don't you leave me."

Against her own will, tears began to stream down her face. She was breaking down, and she could feel it.

Ieshia was just turning to do another bout of pacing when she caught a glimpse of something that was very troubling through the door's large glass window. Four men were passing by out in the hallway. None of the men saw her, but she had seen them and there was no mistaking who they were. They were the four men that had been with Tommy when Jacob had been beaten.

She rushed to the window and peered out at them. All four of them had stopped and was talking to one of the nurses. Staring at them, Ieisha thought that they looked both distressed about something and mentally worn-down. She wondered what it might be, and why they were at the same hospital as she.

For several minutes they conversed, and then the nurse rushed off in a hurry. Each man looked around irritated, causing Ieisha to jump back behind the door, afraid that they might see her. She waited several seconds, and then peeked back out to see if they were still there.

They were gone.

Sighing in relief, she strolled back over to the couch that she'd been sitting on when the elderly woman had comforted her and wrapped her arms around herself. Her nerves completely shot, she began rocking herself back and forth, until she silently cried herself to sleep.

25

Curtis pulled out of his driveway and immediately took notice of the amount of rain that was beginning to fill up all of the gutters, which was causing the streets to begin to flood. It was apparent to him that the weatherman's predictions were correct, and they were about to undergo one terrible storm. He couldn't believe that an actual hurricane was about to hit the state of New Jersey. Actually, he didn't want to believe it, because there was too much going on in his life at the present for him to tolerate anymore turmoil. Plus, there was also the fact that he had no idea where Lamont was, and whether or not his brother was somewhere safe, and seeking shelter.

Never mind the fact that Lamont had taken his Dodge Charger without asking him, after he'd just total-lost one of his other vehicles. The car was a material expense; his little brother wasn't expendable.

Despite Lamont's mishaps, Curtis loved him unconditionally. He was supposed to…his brother was all that he had to remember their biological parents by.

He had to find Lamont before the storm reached its fullest potential. Only then would he feel more confident and secure going after his enemies, because he wouldn't have to worry about his brother getting hurt in the process. Now, if he weren't able to find Lamont, then that would be an entirely different story, because he'd still have to go after Officer Sims and Tommy just to keep reign of his empire. There was no avoiding either of those nuisances. They had to be dealt with. It was the only way that they'd go away. A fight with the two of them was inevitable.

As far as the situation with Tommy went, Curtis knew that the two of them were at the point of no return. Too much blood had been shed and too much pain had been caused. One of them was going to be pushing up daises real soon. Curtis felt with certainty that that someone wouldn't be him.

Officer Sims on the other hand, was a problem. He was a damn cop. How in the hell was he supposed to get away with killing a cop? The dirty motherfucker was going to take more effort to get rid of then Curtis was hoping for.

Why does life have to get so difficult? He wondered.

It was supposed to be about making money and being able to provide for your family, living merry without all of the strife and conflict.

As of now, Curtis' theory of it all seemed to be at its total opposite. Oh, true enough he was making a great deal of money, but the part about living merry was nearly nonexistent. Because of his way life he was at a constant war with an opposing drug cartel that, as the days grew shorter and the nights began to get colder, was only getting worse by the minute. He couldn't even reside under the same roof as his significant other and child, for fear of his hostile conflict reaching Denise's doorstep.

All moves made on his end had to be precise. Every decision that was decided upon had to be pondered over for more time than the average person should have had to contemplate, which in the end was nothing more than a headache that he could have done without.

It was never-ending; which was exactly why Curtis wanted out somewhere in the near future. It was exactly why he'd become so upset when he'd found out that Lamont had begun indulging in the lifestyle as well. He was certain that if his little brother knew the degree of the pain that he dealt with on a daily basis, Lamont would run from the thought of dealing heroin, and wouldn't look back. Most all appealing things looked enticing when you were watching from the outside looking in. Then came the day when you had to actually taste your piece of the pie that you'd asked for.

The streets were bitter, and the people in them could be as cold as a wintry blizzard. The same indigenous pleasures that made you smile could make your teeth chatter in discomforting anguish all in the exact same breath. It wasn't a way of life for just anyone to take a shot at. The weak diminished, while the strong survived.

Curtis knew that he had to put an end to things, and he had to do it soon. Only then, when it was all over with, would he be able to take his family and the fortune that he'd managed to accumulate and get the hell out of dodge. Paterson was his beloved hometown, but it was time for a change. He had to relocate before he did reach a point of no return.

As he drove with caution through the disastrous weather, headed into the direction of West Paterson with the intentions of making a stop at Party City to pick up a few items before going to finish up things with his enemies, he made a mental note to stop by the hospital in Clifton to check up on Jacob's condition.

He wasn't too familiar with Jake's girlfriend, Ieisha, but he was certain that she'd more than likely need someone else's support.

Coming around a curve in the road, Curtis slowed down even more than what he'd already been driving to ensure that he made it around the bend without any accidental mishaps. When he finally made his way completely around it, he came to an intersection that opened up into a two-lane route that would take him directly to his destination.

There was an overhead traffic light flashing red, so he stopped to make certain that he'd have a safe passage, before continuing any further.

Looking straight ahead, he had to squint in order to see a bit more clearer through the downpour. It was nearly impossible for him to see any further than fifteen feet out in front of him.

Gently placing his foot on the accelerator, he cruised forward with precaution. The water level on this side of town was seemingly much higher than that of the flooded streets that he'd already driven through. Here, it just about covered the entire height of his custom rims and tires. He was nearly completely across when something up ahead caught his attention and forced him to stop. He didn't know exactly what it was, but from where he sat it appeared to be an overturned vehicle.

Curtis blinked, then widening his eyes, he strained them to see if he could see a bit further.

"What the hell?" he said growing suspicious.

It was indeed an overturned vehicle. Reaching over into the passenger seat, he grabbed ahold of the poncho that he'd snatched up before leaving his house and pulled it over his head. Donning it, he climbed out in a hurry hoping to minimize the water intake inside his vehicle. The large repellant boots that he wore came three inches above his knees and kept his feet dry, along with the rest of his body.

Tapping his right hip out of habit, he checked to make sure that his sidearm was still in place. Trudging through the muddy-like rainwater, he made his way toward the wrecked vehicle that was blocking his passage and in two dozen strides, he reached it and stared unbelievingly at the license plate of the Chevy Impala that he'd seen Officer Sims driving only hours before.

With mixed emotions, he wondered if he should even check to see if the bastard was still inside. He figured that it wouldn't matter if he was, anyhow, because depending on how long he'd already been inside he was more than likely dead by now. If that were the case, then a ton of pressure would be lifted off of his shoulders.

Looking back toward his vehicle to make certain that it was still idling where he'd left it, Curtis sighed and made the decision to have a look inside of the unmarked car's interior. He could still see the door handles, so one by one he went around checking to see if any of them were unlocked. They weren't. Staring down into the water, he had the urge to stick his head under its surfaced to take a look, but he knew without even having to do so that it was too murky for him to see anything. Looking through that amount of filthy water would be like trying to see through a pool full of diluted chocolate milk.

"Damn it..." he said with annoyance, wishing that he could confirm the crooked cop's death.

Glancing all around himself with the hope of maybe spotting the man floating face down somewhere, something else caught his eye. About sixty meters out lie a ditch that appeared to be several feet deep, from where he stood. He was able to make this assumption because protruding from it was the tail end of another vehicle, its caution lights flashing. The rear of the car was suspended in the air, so he was unable to make its model, or see the plate numbers for that matter.

In a hurry, he sloshed his way into that direction. The closer that he got to the vehicle, the more that he felt he was about to stumble upon something very bad. He reached the car and for a second his heart stopped beating inside of his chest. It was his Dodge Charger.

"Shit...Shit! Shit! Shit! Shit!" he exclaimed, and against his own will, Curtis began to panic.

"Lamont!" he began yelling. "Lamont!"

The water inside of the gully was already about five-foot-deep, and at the rate that it was raining it wouldn't be long before it rose higher. It was useless to try and glance through any of the car's windows, because they were all submerged as well.

"Lamont!" he called out again.

There was a sound...he thought that he heard someone yelling out to him. With his hands bracing the rear bumper, he leaned forward and listened with intent.

He heard it again.

"Lamont..." he nearly screamed, "I'm coming to get you, little bruh!"

Never minding his own safety, he got a good grip on the Charger's bumper and used all of the strength that he had in him to hoist himself up onto the trunk. It took him several seconds before he managed to do so, and when he finally did, he stared down into the rear windshield and could see his brother and a Caucasian female trapped inside.

For a split second, he wondered who the girl was, because she looked vaguely familiar, but the thought passed, and he began to think of ways to get the both of them out.

"Curtis…Curtis, you have to hurry and get us out of here, man!' he heard Lamont yell out to him.

"I'm gonna get y'all out of there, bruh, just hold on!" he assured.

"Come on…think," he told himself.

Reaching for his hip, he thought about shooting the rear windshield out, but then thought better of it. There was a metal Louisville Slugger inside of his trunk.

"Lamont, can you hear me?" he yelled.

His brother nodded.

"I'll be right back, aiight?!"

Lamont nodded again, and Curtis watched as his younger brother took ahold of the Caucasian female's hand.

With one last glance back at them, Curtis turned and jumped back down off the car. Water splashed high into his face and he nearly slipped and went under. Regaining his balance, he moved forward. Making it back to Officer Sims' overturned car, he was just about to pass by the rear of it, when an SUV came zooming into his direction. He watched in disbelief as a Ford Explorer came to a jerking halt beside his car, and a lone man jumped out of the driver-side with a very large gun in his hand.

26

Having taken off from his home without preparing himself for the disastrous storm that had arrived, Tommy's clothes were immediately soaked only seconds after he'd jumped out of his vehicle. His entire body was wet, and the attire that he wore was plastered to him like a second skin. He looked like a madman standing there in the thigh-high water. The barrel of the gun that he held touched the water's surface, as it dangled in his hand. He was breathing heavily, and for several seconds he and Curtis just stared at one another. They were only twenty feet apart and could actually feel the level of hostility between one another . It was an unbelievable feeling of death.

Curtis was about to speak, but Tommy beat him to it. He yelled over the sound of the rain.

"I hope that you're ready to die here, today, Klick Klak, because I am!"

"Hey... look, Tommy, I..."

Curtis never got to finish his sentence, because with a sweep of his arm, Tommy raised his weapon and began firing.

Caught off guard, Curtis had to run for cover. Water splashed around him, as he scurried behind Officer Sims' overturned car and ducked down as low as possible. Snatching his gun free, he held it shoulder level and prepared himself to return fire.

There was a series of shots that rang out, and the bullets that actually managed to stay above water level could be heard smacking into the Chevy Impala's exterior.

Curtis had to think, and fast. He had no time to waste with the water level continuing to rise, because Lamont and his companion were still trapped inside of his other vehicle. Returning fire would only make matters worse, and would prolong the situation, which was definitely not something that he could afford to let happen.

"Come out, coward?" he heard Tommy yell, and then more shots followed. "You want to blow up my fucking spot with grenades? You started this fucking war, you and your brother...but I'm gonna finish it! Now, come out and die like a man, motherfucker!"

"Tommy...you know that your sister's death was an accidental! My brother didn't mean for that to happen!" Curtis tried reasoning.

"Oh, yeah, then what about my man, Tony? Y'all hit my man and his girl up with a fucking grenade!"

"Hey, you and your people warranted that shit! You came on my side of town and done some serious harm to one of mine... your own fucking cousin, man! That shit was foul!"

Out of anger, Tommy fired three more shots, and then paused to reload his weapon.

Unable to think clearly, he gave Curtis the drop on him.

In a flash, Curtis stood from behind the car and high stepped as fast as he could toward Tommy. His gun was aimed, but it was impossible for him to keep his arm steady as he fought his way through the water.

Glancing up, Tommy's eyes grew wide. He tried to hurry and slide the fresh magazine into the pistol that he held, but the closer that Klick Klak got to him, the more that he began to panic. In desperation, he tried to ram the clip inside of the gun, but lost his handle on it and the magazine slipped from his grip and sank into the water.

He looked down as it disappeared and when he glanced back up, an expression of defeat covered his face. He didn't even try to take cover; he only wondered why Klick Klak wasn't firing.

He let his gun slip into the water as well and baring his teeth, he shut his eyes. Several seconds passed before he realized that nothing was happening, so he opened them, only to find Curtis standing before him.

There was no longer a gun in Klick Klak's hand, and Tommy took this as a sign that his adversary wished to brawl it out.

He put up his hands and balled them into fists. "Hey…" Curtis said pointing his finger in Tommy's face, "what don't you understand? I don't want any beef with you!"

Tommy just looked at him as if he'd gone crazy. "I don't want to keep going to war with you, man. I'm tired of this shit, and you should be too. This bullshit over some fucking territory and drug money ain't worth dying over, nor is it worth killing someone over.

I told you that I'm sorry about your sister, Tommy, and I mean that. I'm taking all of this as a sign… I'm getting out of the game, man…for good. So, if you want the streets, then you can have them, because I'm done. I don't want anymore of the stress… the pain… or the death that comes along with the game. I can't take it anymore… I'm sick of this shit!"

Pulling the gun free that he'd tucked inside of his waistband, Curtis looked down at it, and then back up at Tommy. He thought deeply for a second, and then came to a realization that if life was really all about pain and no love, then he wasn't willing to allow himself to have to suffer on this earth any longer. His brother was several yards away trapped inside of a luxury vehicle that he'd bought using some of the dope money that he'd earned, while he stood pleading with a man that wanted to see him dead. If he and Lamont were going to die, then on all that he loved they would die together.

Taking one last glance back into the direction where Lamont and his female friend were waiting for him to come back and save them, he turned back to face Tommy and held the gun out to him with its handle first.

Tommy's eyes grew wide.

"My little brother is over there trapped inside of that vehicle, and if I don't get back over there in the right amount of time, then he's going to drown," Curtis told him.

Tommy's head angled into the direction in which Curtis had just implicated, and his eyes roamed over the Dodge Charger that was apparently stuck inside of the ditch.

"I know that you blame him for your sister's death, but Tommy I can assure you that he is truly sorry, because he didn't mean for that accident to happen."

Tommy snatched the gun from Curtis, and his chest began to rise and fall at an unnerving rate. He said nothing.

Taking a step backward and preparing himself, Curtis expected the worst to come fast.

"If my brother's going to die, Tommy... then I'm going to die with him. He's all that I have," he said with resignation.

They stared into one another's eyes for what seemed like an eternity; one man appearing calm, while the other seemed maddened beyond reason.

This is it, Curtis thought, unaware of his own tears as they slid down his face. I'm sorry, Lamont...I tried.

He watched as Tommy breathed heavily, looking back and forth from where they stood to where Curtis brother sat trapped, and just when he thought that the man was about to raise the gun and put an end to all of his problems, his adversary's breathing became normal again, and his hand let go of the weapon.

Tommy took a step closer to Curtis so that were standing face to face.

"I didn't think that anyone else could love someone as much as I loved my sister. Let's go and get your brother out of that car, Curtis," Tommy told him.

With one last look into his eyes, Curtis saw that Tommy was sincere and a sense of relief fell over him like something that he'd never felt before. "I have to get a baseball bat out of my trunk," he told Tommy, turning quickly so that he could hurry and retrieve it.

Moving around Tommy's Explorer, he made his way around to his car. Reaching it, he saw that the water was beginning to reach window level, which left the trunk covered entirely. Never minding the fact that his car audio system was about to be damaged, he opened the trunk and snatched the Louisville Slugger out, before all of the filthy water rushed inside.

"I got it!" he said coming back around the car, and meeting Tommy at the frontend of his truck.

"You ready?" Tommy asked him.

"Yeah, let's go," Curtis told him and began to lead the way. It was a little harder getting to the Charger than what it had been the first time, and both Curtis and Tommy had to very careful not to lose their footing. The water was beginning to rise at a rapid pace and had started to take on a current.

They reached the Charger and Curtis turned to Tommy.

"I'm gonna need to you help me climb up on the trunk!"

Tommy nodded, swiping the water from his eyes. Taking a stance, he heaved and helped Curtis up onto the trunk on the first try. The water inside of the ditch had raised so much to the point that it was nearly covering the entire rear windshield, now.

Thankful that he could still see Lamont and his companion moving inside, Curtis raised the bat high over his head and brought it crashing down. Nothing happened the first time, other than a tiny fracture in the glass appearing. He swung it again and got the same result. A third and nothing.

"Come on!" he screamed, breathing heavily.

"Hey, Curt..." he heard Tommy call up to him, "help me climb up there!"

Using his free arm, Curtis did so.

"Let me see that," Tommy told him reaching for the bat, and Curtis relinquished it to him. Looking down into the car, Tommy could see the surprise expression on Lamont's face as he told Curtis, I used to be a designated hitter for Eastside High."

In one swift motion, Tommy brought the Louisville Slugger down with enough force to shatter the entire windshield into a thousand little pieces of diamond-shaped glass. Water rushed into the car and the force of it knocked both Lamont and Bridget back up against the front windshield. For several seconds they struggled to make forward progress. Finally, they were able to swim forward.

Each one of them grabbing ahold of someone's hand, Tommy and Curtis were able to pull the young couple free. There wasn't enough room for all four of them to stand on top of the Charger's trunk, so once they were just about completely all of the way out, both Tommy and Curtis jumped down onto the ground. By now, the water was up to their stomachs.

Glancing up at Lamont and Bridget, Curtis told them that they'd have to jump down as well.

They did so and were caught before they could lose their balance and slip under.

Curtis turned and looked into the direction in which he'd left his car that he'd been driving.

"Shit…" he said seeing that it wasn't far from being completely submerged.

Tommy's truck wasn't as bad off, though.

"Hey, man, y'all can catch a ride with me. This stuff is getting bad, and we have to get out of here," Tommy told them.

They hurried into that direction, fighting their way through the flood. They finally reached the Explorer, and in just a matter of seconds they were all climbing inside.

Checking themselves over to make sure that they'd not sustained any injuries that might have gone unnoticed; they all took a moment to glance at one another in appreciation.

Looking through the rearview mirror, Tommy and Lamont locked eyes.

"I'm very sorry, Tommy…" Lamont said with sincerity.

Tommy just nodded.

"Thank you for saving our lives," Bridget added.

Looking ahead at the mess of a road before them, Tommy sighed, and a sense of relief fell over him. He slid the key into the ignition and crank up the vehicle. At that very moment, something happened to him. Somewhere deep inside his soul a battle between good and evil had been won. All that had once pained him was now nearly nonexistent. There was a strong sense of peace taking over inside of him, and he knew that he could now do something that he'd never known possible. He could forgive.

With one last look at Curtis, he stuck out his hand and called their qualms to a truce.

Curtis accepted the gesture, and told him, "Thank you… you're a good man, Tommy. You now have a brother in me."

That said, Tommy put the truck into drive, and slowly brought the vehicle up to a reasonable speed, just as his cell phone rang and revealed his home phone number.

It was his baby, Stephanie calling.

27

The door to the intensive care unit's waiting area opened quietly, and a doctor accompanied by his scrub nurse stepped inside the room. Taking one look at the sleeping woman told them exactly what they had already assumed; the poor woman had been worrying sick over her boyfriend that had flat-lined earlier that day. They were certain that the sight of her lover dying in the manner in which he had, had been painfully traumatizing for the young lady, because it was apparent that she was in love with the man that had been very badly beaten. Because his heart had stopped, they'd had to react quickly. Once they'd managed to revive him, they'd discovered that he'd had severe internal bleeding in his chest area and had been forced to perform an immediate operation on him. Luckily for the young lady that lay dozing in a fetal position on one of the sofas, her boyfriend had been strong enough to pull through.

They approached her quietly, and the doctor laid a gentle hand on the woman's shoulder.

"Excuse me, Miss…" he said in an attempt to rouse her. She stirred, but her eyes remained shut.

"Uh, Miss… you can wake up, now… come on, young lady," he said nudging her shoulder.

Ieisha's eyes fluttered open and at first sight of the doctor and his nurse, she sat up with a start. It had been hours since she'd last eaten, and in her weakened state she swayed on her feet when she tried to stand.

"Whoa…" the female nurse said catching her in her arms, "take it easy."

Taking a better look at her, now, the doctor could see that she was actually a very pretty woman, but the stress that she was under was causing her to look a bit haggard.

"Are you okay, Miss?" he asked.

Ieisha just nodded, while brushing her hair away from her face. The nurse had yet to turn her completely loose.

"Are you sure?" he asked.

"Yes…I'm alright," she told him, although she had been anticipating this moment for hours, and feared what news he might be bringing. She wondered if they would have waited this long to inform her of Jacob's condition if he had died.

Willing herself to stand on her own, Ieisha pulled away from the woman's hold, and faced the doctor with an inquiring look.

Taking note of the woman's strength, he smiled.

That kid lying in that bed sure is a lucky man, he thought.

"Jacob is fine, Miss…he's resting in recovery right now as we speak," he told her, and he watched as her eyes began to mist over. It was obvious that she was overcome with joy, because she clasped her hands together and brought them up to her face in a silent prayer.

When she was done, she dropped her hands and allowed her tears to run freely.

"Thank you, doctor…thank you so much," she told him, grabbing ahold of his hand and shaking it gently.

"Can I see him?" she asked.

"Yes, of course…" he said, and with a consoling hand on her back, he ushered her from the depressing confinements of the waiting room, and down the corridor that would lead them to Jacob.

Rayshawn, Kwalib, Shahid, and Talil all felt relief as they strolled through the lobby of the hospital headed for an exit that would lead them out to their car. All four men were ready to remove themselves from the confinements of the charitable institution. They'd been inside of the building for hours now, after having rushed and demanded that Tony receive immediate care. Fearing that their eldest leader had been critically injured during the malicious assault earlier on while they'd been clocking on their block, they'd been persistent with the medical staff and had been fortunate to receive some cooperation without much convincing.

After what had seemed like an entire day full of test, the doctor had come to inform them that their friend had only suffered a concussion, accompanied by some minor cuts and bruises. There had also been a small amount of shrapnel that had made its way beneath Tony's scalp, and had actually been the cause of all the blood that he'd been covered with. Sadly, from what they'd been told, his girlfriend hadn't been as lucky he. Whereas he'd just suffer a few bad headaches once he awakened, she would never have the chance to see the sun rise again, because she'd been killed in the blast. Nearly blown to pieces.

Since they were all now for certain that Tony would be alright and would pull through with a full recovery, they figured that they should probably be getting back to the block to make sure that his shop was getting put back in order. Because they had not known the exact whereabouts of Tommy, Shahid had had to make the call to head back. They were going to have to go and see what the government officials were up to out there, and what they had managed to uncover. There was no doubt that their operation had been compromised. Their ensuing war between themselves and Klick Klak's Westside crew had gotten too violent, and they would now face a great deal of scrutiny that hadn't already been there. Someone would ask questions and want to know what had caused this act of deliberate violence to occur. They'd want to know how any mere citizen could have acquired such a weapon of mass destruction like the one that had been used today, which would warrant the presence of the ATF in the end. That group of government officials probably wouldn't leave town for a while, and their main focus would be on the Eastside section of the town where the incident had occurred.

Things were about to get really hectic, but what had to be done had to be done. Until Tony was back on his feet and Tommy resurfaced, someone had to look after the shop.

Approaching the receptionist's desk, all four men waited as Shahid paused to inquire about the next visiting hours for intensive care patients. The middle-age Hispanic woman smiled and kindly told him, "They are from ten a.m. to five p.m."

"Why so late in the morning?" he asked.

"Because it gives the medical staff enough time to prepare the patient for the day." He thanked her and was turning to lead his entourage out into the parking lot, when she stopped him.

"Uh, sir, you can't go out that way," she told him.

"Huh… what do you mean?" he asked, and they all turned to face her with quizzical expressions.

"Those doors are ground level and they're all barricaded on the outside… no one can get out from down here."

"Why?' Shahid asked, and Kwalib stepped up beside him, glaring down at the woman with skepticism.

"Oh, you haven't seen. The parking lot's flooded... the only way out is up through pediatrics, because it's on an uphill. Even then you're limited to how far you can get out into the city."

"You're kidding, right?" Shahid asked, and Kwalib stepped up beside him, glaring down at the woman with skepticism.

The woman chuckled and shook her head.

"How long have you all been up there?" she asked.

"A couple of hours," Kwalib answered.

"So, you guys haven't seen how bad the storm has gotten?"

"Shit..." Shahid swore without bothering to answer her question. Several more profanities followed after his. She pointed to a set of stairs that led up to one of the lobby's break room areas, and told them, "hey, go up there inside of that room and take a look out over the street. There are some large windows that will give you a pretty good view of what things out there are looking like." All of them nodded and turning, they headed into that direction. "Hurry, though, because that room is preserved for staff only, and I don't want my boss to catch y'all in there, 'cause then he'll get on my case."

The men kept it moving, and in a matter of seconds they reached the top of the stairs.

Leading the way, Shahid pushed the door to the break room open and they all stepped inside. The room was empty and smelled strongly of fresh lemons and Clorox. Silently, they all walked over to the windows and stood beside one another. No one said anything. They just stared, astonishment getting the best of them.

Just as the woman had informed them, the entire parking area was flooded, as well as the streets below them. It was unbelievable how much water was trapped on the ground's surface, and it was evident to them all that no one was going anywhere for some time. It would probably even be days before they could get out of there. They were indeed stuck until the stormed passed.

Epilogue

By the late evening that day the storm had finally reached its fullest potential. Like nothing seen before, it assaulted the city of Paterson with enough turbulent force that the level of destruction that it was causing was rapidly surpassing that of the late Hurricane Hugo.

The winds that blew were nearly unbearable to withstand. The water level had risen to unbelievably large heights. Never before had there been this much rainwater trapped on the earth's surface where large bodies of water were an irregularity. There were motor vehicles that had been abandoned floating without direction, or wherever the current would drag them. Homes and businesses were submerged in seven-foot-deep murky water. Local schools had evacuated, and those that had been fortunate enough to seek refuge in a safe place took their families and did so. Some were lucky enough to receive assistance from the local authorities, while others were left to fend for themselves.

It was a very trying period for many the day that Hurricane Irene arrived. It would take a lot for the people of the city to rebuild their beloved town back up to the living standards that they were accustomed to. Whether or not they'd able to set aside their typical day to day differences would be the determining factor on how long it would actually take them to see some progress. Disaster didn't care what race you were, or what your creed was. It cared not about what gender you were, or your sexual preference, because when it arrived it came hard and unrelenting; all was game under its indiscriminate destruction. Nothing else mattered.

So, as the storm was without prejudice, so would the people that had endured it have to be, once it passed.

For some, Hurricane Irene was proving to be the most critical trial that they'd undergone in life. As it exceeded anything that they'd ever been faced with, it had given them a testament that would prove worthy to be told somewhere in the future, and for a very longtime after.

For young street-oriented people like Curtis and Tommy, it was an eye-opener. Before Irene's arrival, both had been only minutes away from total self-destruction. Had it not been for the demanding effects of the storm, there would have probably been an increasing number of onslaughts between the two and their entourages, especially after the accidental death of Tommy's sister, Alaena. The term retaliation would have probably taken on an entirely different meaning.

Because of Irene, the drug trade in Paterson would never be the same. The illegal distribution of narcotics had suffered a major hit, because the hearts of the men that had once regulated the streets had now changed. It wasn't a long stint in some form of judiciary confinement that had caused either of the gentlemen to see the bigger picture either, nor was it vicious robbery that is sometimes the cause of a kingpin losing his vital place on his throne that made things different. Those factors weren't even close to the truth. Some things were just meant to come to an end, while others were preparing to begin. In Buddha they called it balance.

The storm that ravished the entire East Coast that year not only brought disaster, but it brought balance as well. There had been chaos, whereas in many ways Irene had brought peace.

Although, the town's visible appearance was a total mess and in disarray, internally, the souls of its residents were being redeemed. They were turning to one another for help; whether lending it, or in need. They were praying for each other, feeding the homeless, protecting their fellow man, and nurturing their feeblish women and children. Strong women were working with men side by side, while the disabled were relentless in finding a way to contribute to their efforts.

If someone were to have recorded it all on video, it would have looked to many as if this were exactly what a town like Paterson had needed. If the cost of returning love back into someone's heart was the price of losing their home, then it's certain that those that had already lost many relatives dear to them before the storm would have preferred that a natural disaster arrive more frequently.

It was truly a miracle to see everyone working together as they were; a sight to remember and a moment to cherish. Who would have thought that such a thing could ever occur?

When all was said and done, Curtis would more than likely move in with Denise and their daughter permanently. Lamont, thank goodness, would be going off to college to play both football and basketball at one of the Division 2 schools that he'd received a scholarship from, although, not without first convincing Curtis to send Bridget along with him.

As for Tommy, his story would be a bit more exciting, since he and Stephanie would finally be getting married; especially now that Stephanie was with child, although, she didn't know it yet. The newly wedded mother would open up a daycare, so that she'd be able to spend her entire working day with she and Tommy's newborn.

Tommy's business adventures would turn out to be another testament to the 'hood, because surprisingly to many, he and Curtis were opening up a recreational center for boys and girls. They were going to name it after Tommy's late sister, Alaena. Curtis' declaration to Tommy would prove to be authentic. He was going to be the brother that Tommy never had. Life had gone from one ugly mirage, to the most beautiful pictorial moments that the city of Paterson had ever seen. And although, most people believe in the saying that 'life is what you make it', in the case of 'One-Two Live' and 'The D-Pound Crew, none of this would have ever been possible, I believe… Until Irene.

The End

Dear Reader,

I'd like to begin by first thanking you for taking the time to read my first published work. I truly hope that you enjoyed the story, and its characters. God willing, there will be more to come in the very near future.

I first wrote this story several years ago, but because of some abrupt current life changing events, which occurred on August 4th, 2020, when a tornado swept through Windsor, NC, at approximately 01:30am and claimed the lives of two of my neighbors, I lost my home to a tornado that was caused by Hurricane Isaias. Isaias ripped my entire home from its foundation and turned everything in it, and around it into rubble. Luckily, God was there to protect my family and made sure we made a way to have a better life than before.

I'd never been this close to such a violent tropical storm, so having one literally hit home was nearly mind-shattering. For several days I was traumatized by the sight of the destruction that Hurricane Isaias caused. The few lives that were claimed in Bertie County, North Carolina were heartbreaking, and a wake-up call. Life is too short to dwell in a haze of unhappiness and resentment, and definitely too short not to love, be loved, or live out our dreams. So, with this new encouragement to live and be happy, I am beginning a new journey by digging down within myself and reaching for the best of me to share with all of you.

I hope to encourage those that have experienced some of the same as I have to do the same. Just as well I'd like to give a special thanks to the County of Bertie and all of its supporters for the grave efforts that they've put in to help all of our families rebuild both their homes and lives, as well as my loving fiancé. I will forever be grateful and encouraged by all of you.

With love,
A'taris Anthony

Made in the USA
Middletown, DE
28 September 2022